Five reasons why you'll fall in love with Nixie!

- Bumblebees' Bottoms! Nixie's always getting in trouble!
- A completely new kind of fairy in fairyland.
- Rainbow Fairies meets Horrid Henry!
- Full of magical mishaps and ingenious inventions!
- A wonderfully funny story, packed with gorgeous illustrations.

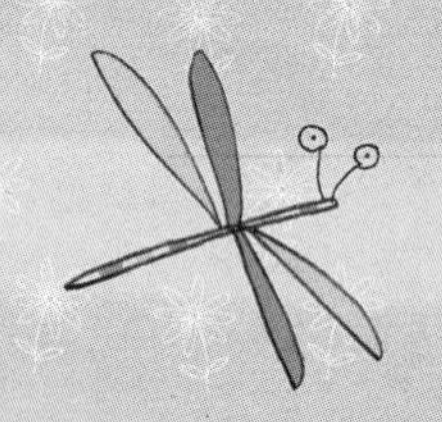

We love Nixie!

'Fantastically funny book . . . Loved it!'
independentbookreviews.co.uk

'Great for any young reader who's more interested in mischief than frill, glitter and staying spotless.'
Helen Mulley, Teach Primary

'Full of fun and magical mischief'
Armadillo Magazine

'I think everybody should read this book because it's really funny'
Kid Around magazine

Getting to know Nixie!

Nixie is brilliant at lots of things—but there are loads of things she's not very good at!

Three things Nixie is BRILLIANT at :

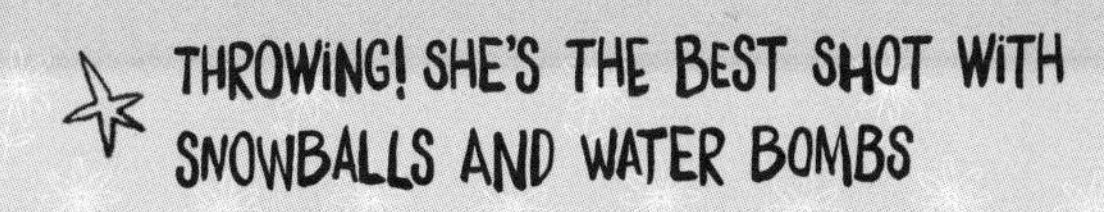

- THROWING! SHE'S THE BEST SHOT WITH SNOWBALLS AND WATER BOMBS
- INVENTING THINGS
- MAKING UP GAMES

Three things Nixie is RUBBISH at:

- BOTTOM-SITS ON THE TRAMPOLINE
- KEEPING OUT OF TROUBLE
- GETTING HER WONKY WAND TO DO WHAT SHE WANTS IT TO DO

For Julia,
who always believed in Nixie – Cas

For everyone at St Stephen's School,
Twickenham – Ali

OXFORD
UNIVERSITY PRESS

Great Clarendon Street, Oxford OX2 6DP

Oxford University Press is a department of the University of Oxford.
It furthers the University's objective of excellence in research, scholarship,
and education by publishing worldwide. Oxford is a registered trademark of
Oxford University Press in the UK and in certain other countries

First published 2016

British Library Cataloguing in Publication Data

Data available

ISBN: 978-0-19-274485-2

1 3 5 7 9 10 8 6 4 2

Printed in Great Britain by Bell and Bain Ltd, Glasgow

Paper used in the production of this book is a natural,
recyclable product made from wood grown in sustainable forests.
The manufacturing process conforms to the environmental
regulations of the country of origin.

Nixie

Splashy Summer Swim

Cas Lester

Illustrated by Ali Pye

OXFORD
UNIVERSITY PRESS

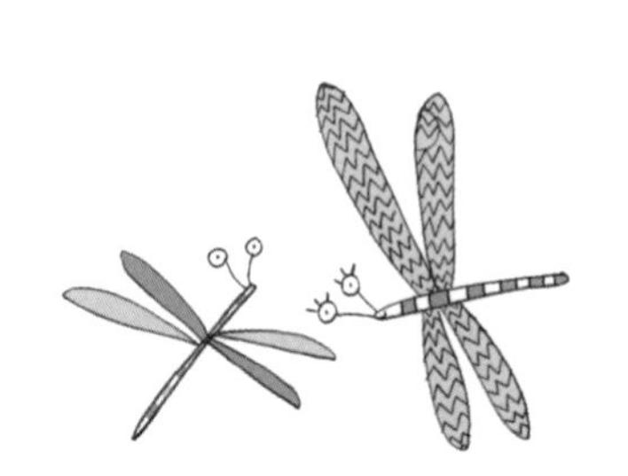

Contents

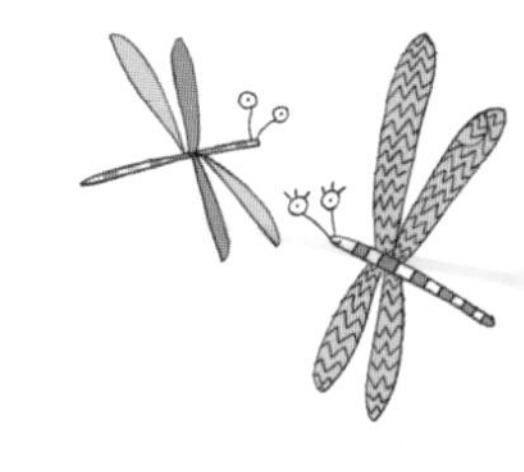

Chapter 1

BOUNCY BOTTOM-SITS

BOING, BOUNCE, SPLAT!

'Bumblebees' bottoms! I can't do it!' groaned Nixie the Bad, Bad Fairy. She'd just landed in a crumpled heap on a cobweb, with her bottom in the air—for the umpteenth time that morning.

Nixie's friends roared with laughter.

'You nearly did it,' grinned Fizz the Wish Fairy.

It was a brilliantly hot summer day and they were trampolining on a cobweb, seeing how many bottom-sits they could do. Twist the Cobweb Fairy was ahead with fifteen. Fidget the Butterfly Fairy and Fizz the Wish Fairy had both done eleven.

But Nixie was hopeless! She kept ending up sprawled across the cobweb with her big red clompy

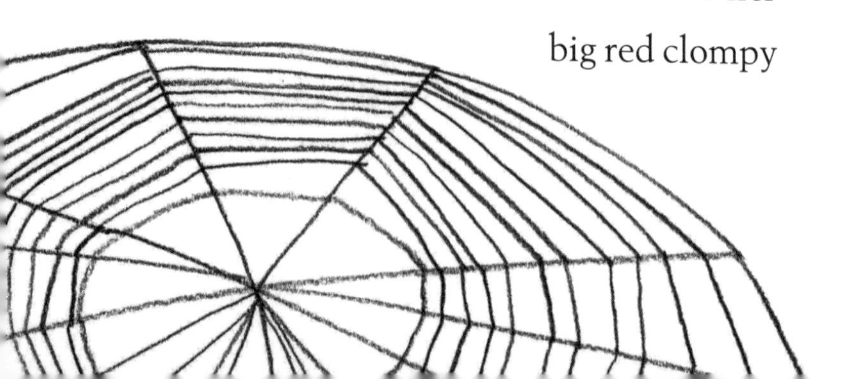

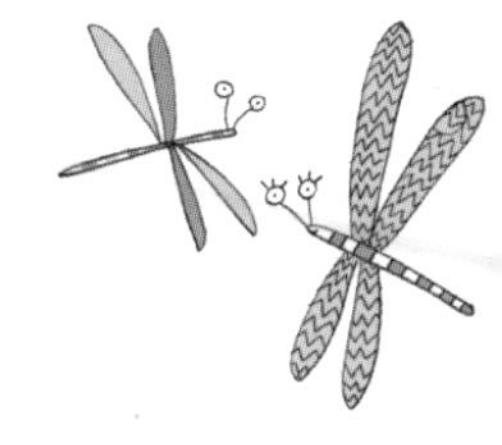

boots all tangled up.

'Try again,' cried Fidget.

'But bounce higher!' called Twist.

Nixie's little black wings buzzed in concentration, and her grubby little face frowned.

BOUNCE . . . BOING . . .

Her tatty dress flashed bright red in the clear blue sky as she jumped super-high.

'Here goes!' she yelled, but . . .

BOING, BOUNCE, SPLAT!

'Ooof!' she gasped, landing flat on her back with her legs waggling in the air.

Everyone fell about laughing.

'You're meant to stick your legs out when you sit!' hooted Fidget.

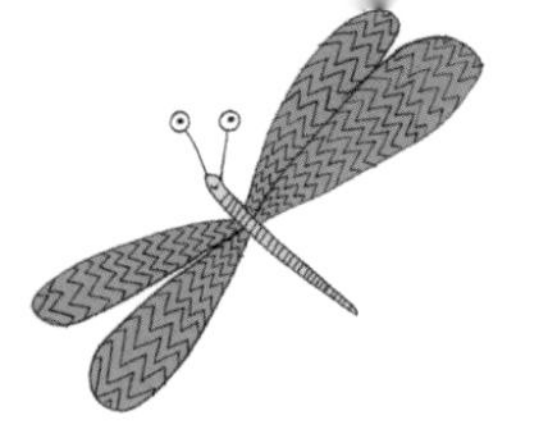

'I can't!' exclaimed Nixie, 'Not in these great big boots!'

'Well, take them off,' suggested Fizz.

But Nixie didn't want to take her boots off. It was where she kept her fairy wand, and her trusty spanner.

She was very tempted to use her wonky black wand with its wobbly red star, right now, to make her boots smaller. But she couldn't exactly trust her wand to do as it was told. The last time she'd enchanted her boots was at the Blossom Ball, and her mischievous wand had made her boots dance along the table, up the wall, and across the ceiling—while Nixie was still in them and hanging upside down!

'I give up,' she grinned and did some really high bounces instead.

BOING! BOUNCE! BOING!

As she bounced she could see Briar the Flower Fairy and Willow the Tree Fairy watering flowers in the Fairy Glade. It looked like very hot work.

BOUNCE!

Briar had emptied the watering can so Willow was filling it up again from the Twisty Trickle Stream that splashed through the Fairy Glade and down to the Polished Pebble Pond.

BOING!

On the other side of the Fairy Glade, Nixie saw Adorabella the Goody-goody Fairy lying in a patch of daisies, reading a book. It was so hot she was fanning herself with a small leaf.

BOUNCE!

Nixie heard Briar call over to Adorabella. 'Can you come and give us a hand?'

But Adorabella just wafted her leaf and groaned. 'I'm much too hot to do anything!'

BOING!

Nixie bounced up again in time to see Willow and Briar roll their eyes at each other, and then carry on watering.

Huh, typical! thought Nixie, slowing down and bouncing to a standstill. *Why should Adorabella get to laze around, while Briar and Willow do all the work?*

Of course Nixie wasn't actually doing any work either. *But I'd help if they asked me!* she told herself indignantly. *In fact, I think*

I'm going to have to do something about that lazy Adorabella!

'I'm going to help Briar and Willow,' she announced with a wicked gleam in her green eyes, and she darted up off the trampoline and flew to the Fairy Path.

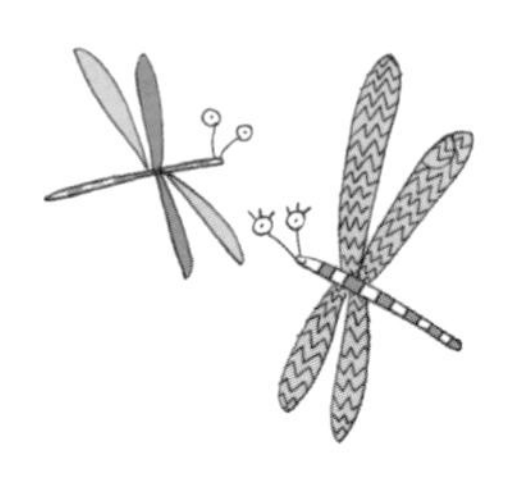

Briar and Willow had been watering all morning. They'd done the daisies that grew **higgledy-piggledy** around the grass and now they were giving the flowers along the **zigzag** Fairy Path a much needed drink. The plants were wilting

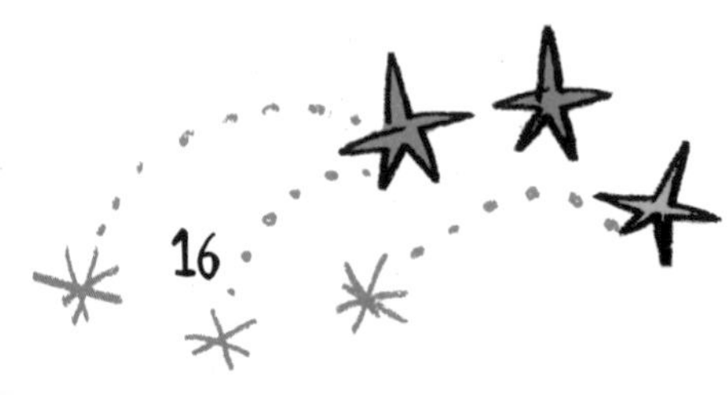

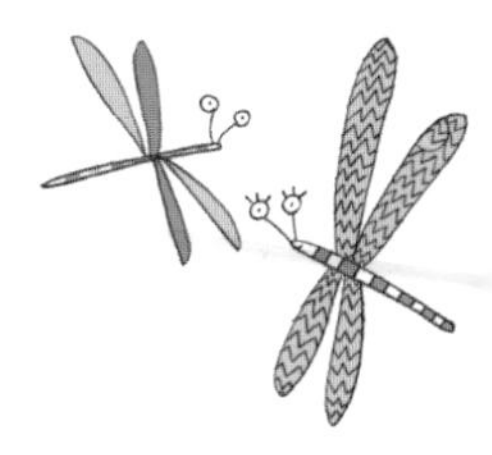

in the heat—and so were the fairies! So when Nixie flitted down asking to help, Briar gladly handed her the watering can.

'Is there lots of nice **cold** water in it?' asked Nixie.

'Yes, I've just filled it from the stream,' said Willow.

'Good!' grinned Nixie. And, being careful not to make any noise, she tiptoed over to where Adorabella was sunbathing in the daisies.

Very quietly, she watered a bluebell, and then she watered a daisy . . . and finally she watered Adorabella—by emptying the entire contents of the watering can over her!

There was a huge **SPLOSH!**
And a piercing **SCREAM!**

Chapter 2

THE FAIRY GODMOTHER'S DAY OFF

Adorabella was drenched! Her hair was plastered flat, her frilly yellow fairy dress soaked through, and water dribbled off her wings.

'Ooops! Sorry,' laughed Nixie. 'I didn't see you there!'

'Yes you did! You did that on purpose!'

shrieked Adorabella.

'Did not! I was watering the daisies!' lied Nixie, shamelessly.

'You big fat **hairy-fairy fibber!**' yelled Adorabella. 'I'm telling the Fairy Godmother on you,' and she darted off. Willow and Briar were desperately trying not to laugh out loud.

'You'd better go and say sorry,' giggled Briar, taking the watering can back.

'Otherwise you'll get in trouble with the Fairy Godmother,' grinned Willow.

Nixie sighed and zipped off after Adorabella.

Tabitha Quicksilver, the Fairy Godmother, was lying on a sunlounger under a stripy

purple-and-white umbrella by the side of the Polished Pebble Pond. It was her day off and she was flicking through a pile of magazines she hadn't had a moment to read. She had last month's *Star Dust*

Secrets, two copies of *Wands and Wishes Weekly,* a *What's on in Fairyland,* and her favourite, *Sparkle!*

She couldn't remember the last time she'd sat down for more than five minutes without having to deal with some crisis or other in Fairyland. Often caused by Nixie . . . well, almost always, in fact.

Like the time Nixie turned the royal coach into a bubble and it blew away—with the Fairy Queen inside! And when she turned the Fairy Godmother herself into a cupcake with pink icing and a cherry on top! Tabitha Quicksilver **shuddered** at the memory.

She leant against the soft cushion, gazed at

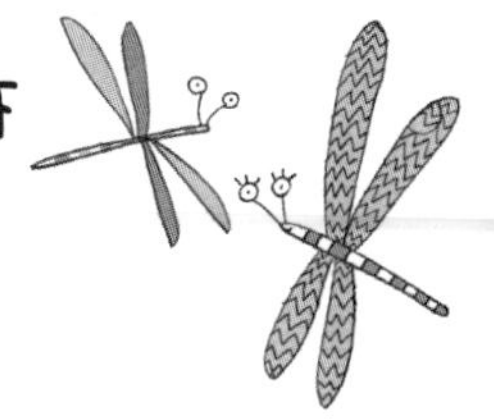

the pond, and sighed contentedly. It looked particularly pretty today with **sparkles** of sunlight dancing on the surface under the clear blue summer sky. The trees and grass growing round the edge **shimmered** bright green in the soft breeze.

Picking up her copy of *Sparkle!* she flicked through to a picture story about the Enchanted Palace and settled down to read.

It was a very hot day, so most of the fairies wanted to swim in the pond. Buzby, the Fairy Godmother's little honeybee assistant, was busily trying to sort them

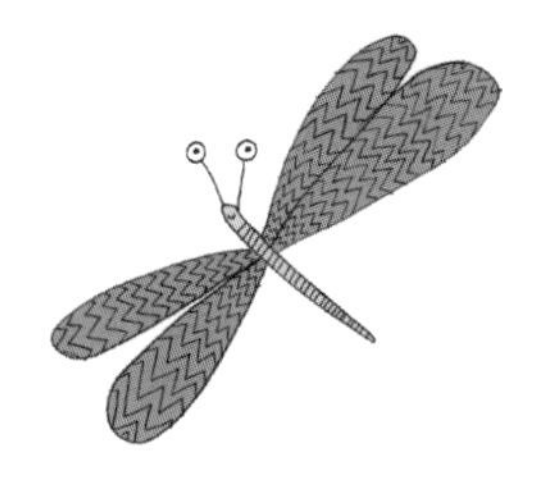

all out with armbands and goggles and rubber rings. But everything was in an enormous muddle! It was hard to know where to begin!

He started by trying to match the armbands into pairs. There were orange ones and yellow ones, a blue one with fishes on, and a red and white spotted one.

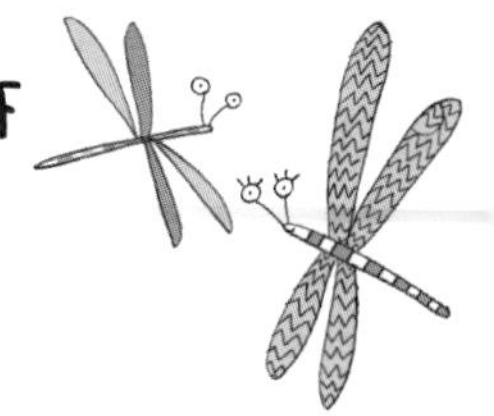

When he'd finally sorted the armbands as best he could, he began to blow them all up.

This was hard work for the little bee because his furry chest didn't have room for a lot of puff inside. Excitedly, the little fairies grabbed the nearest ones and pulled them on. Poor Buzby couldn't keep track of who had what! He waggled his antennae and tut-tutted anxiously.

On the sunlounger, Tabitha Quicksilver was so interested in the photos of the Enchanted Palace that she didn't hear Adorabella fluttering up.

But suddenly . . .

PLIP, PLOP! DRIBBLE, DROP!

'Oooh!' she squealed! Drops of cold water were splattering all over her.

She looked up to see a very sad and soggy Adorabella. 'Adorabella! You're dripping on me!'

'It's not my fault,' cried Adorabella, and she made her bottom lip wobble.

Then, when this didn't seem to have any effect on the Fairy Godmother, she burst into tears instead.

'It was Nixie!' she sobbed.

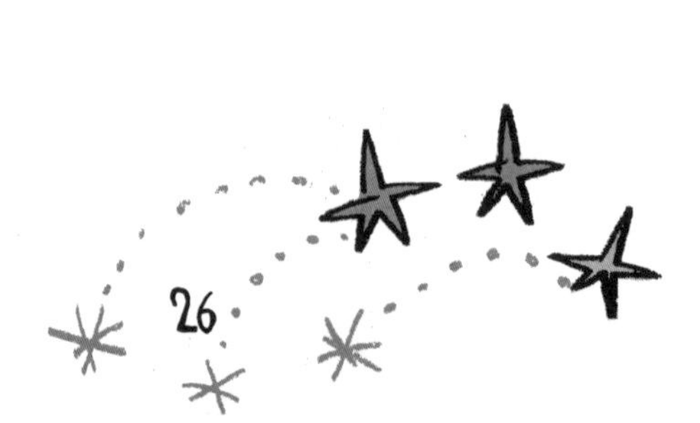

Chapter 3

A Great Big Hairy-Fairy Row

'Whatever happened?' asked Tabitha Quicksilver.

'I was lying in the flowers, sunbathing,' Adorabella snivelled, 'when Nixie crept up and threw a watering can full of freezing cold water all over me, completely on purpose. And now I'm soaked.' She

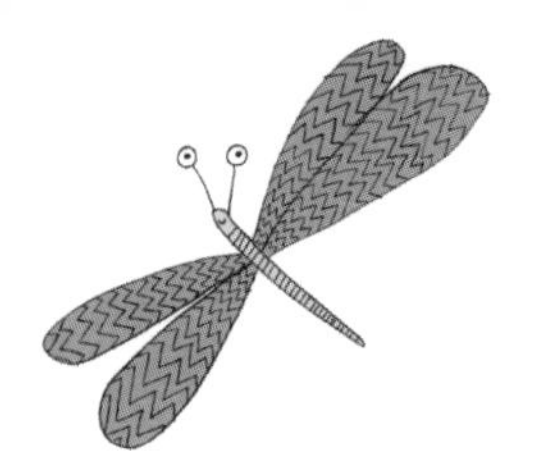

fluttered her wings weakly to show the Fairy Godmother how wet they were.

Just then, Nixie arrived.

'Whatever she says I did, I didn't do it—or at least I didn't mean to!' she fibbed quickly.

The Fairy Godmother gave Nixie a look over the top of her glasses.

'What didn't you do?' she asked, dryly.

Nixie took a deep breath. 'Well, I was helping Briar and Willow water the flowers in the Fairy Glade. So, I was actually being good and doing something useful, when I **accidentally** splashed Adorabella. How was I to know Adorabella was sunbathing in the daisies? **It's not my fault** if some

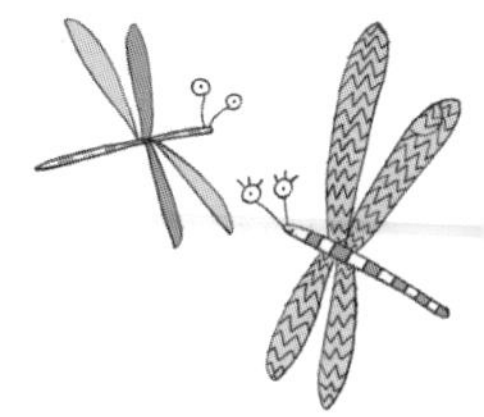

people lie around being lazy in exactly the same place where the rest of us are trying to work.'

'Well, perhaps you should be more careful,' said Tabitha Quicksilver. 'And I think you should say "sorry" to Adorabella.'

'Why?' snorted Nixie. 'It was an accident! And anyhow, she should say "thank you" to me for cooling her down on a hot day!'

Adorabella gasped at Nixie's cheek.

Tabitha Quicksilver took a deep, calming breath.

'Fairies, it's my day off and I'm trying to relax and read. So please just run along and play!'

Sinking back down onto the sunlounger she added, 'And Nixie, try to keep out of mischief!'

'But aren't you going punish her?' pouted Adorabella, folding her arms.

'No,' said the Fairy Godmother. 'I didn't see what happened, and I've only got your word against hers.'

Nixie poked her tongue out at Adorabella and waggled it.

'That's not fairy fair!' wailed Adorabella.

'She's always being horrible to me.'

'No, I'm not!'

'Yes, you are!' retorted Adorabella, truthfully.

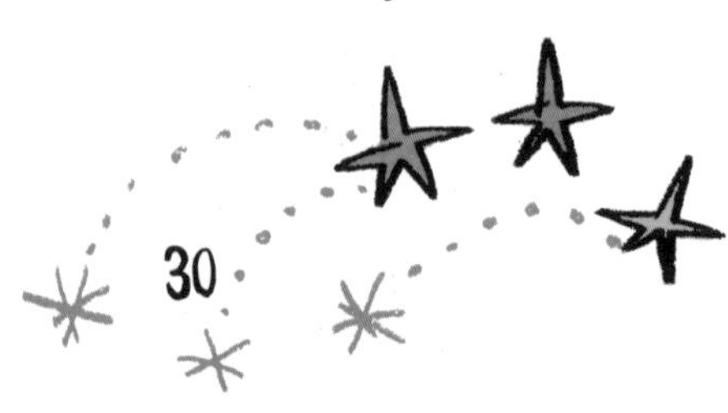

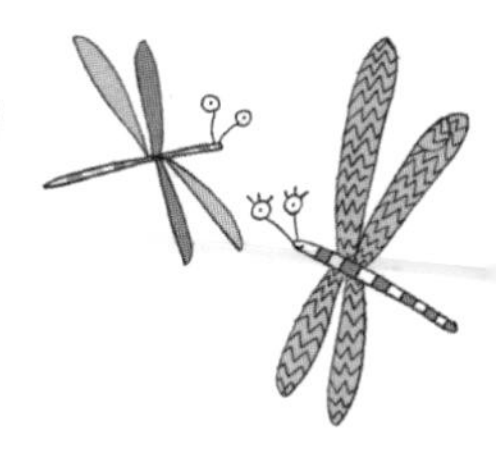

'Am not!'

'Yesterday you turned my magic wand into an ice lolly and it nearly melted away!'

Nixie snorted with laughter.

'FAIRIES! It's far too hot for this! Why don't you both go and cool off in the pond?' Tabitha Quicksilver suggested.

'I'm not playing with Nixie!' sulked Adorabella.

'Good!' snorted Nixie, and, stopping only long enough to blow a raspberry at Adorabella, she darted off to fetch her friends.

Adorabella fluttered home to her pretty little wooden fairy house to change into her swimming costume.

Tabitha Quicksilver picked up her magazines again, but they were all damp and the pages had stuck together. She sighed and gave up trying to read.

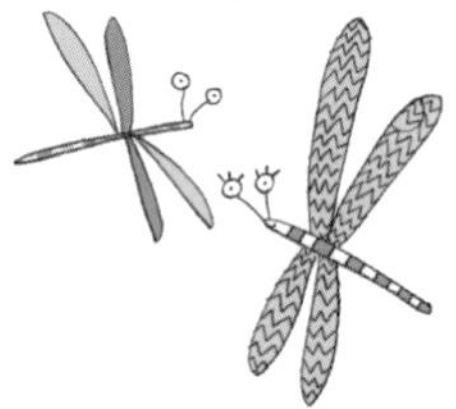

Meanwhile, Buzby was trying to help the fairies put on goggles and snorkles and flippers. But everything was in such a jumble he was finding it tricky to untangle it all. Some of the goggles were broken, one of the snorkels was bent in the middle,

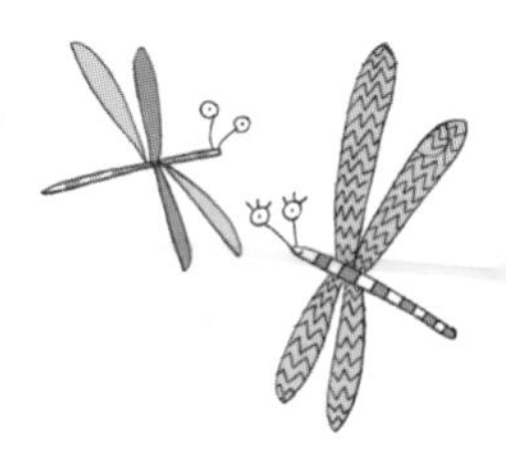

and two pairs of flippers didn't have any straps at all.

The little fairies waited, trying very hard to be patient. But then a couple of them started playing with some long noodle floats, whirling them around their heads. And then some others joined in and a fun float fight broke out!

Buzby, who was already feeling very flustered, buzzed over crossly and took the floats away. Nobody could help themselves to floats, he announced. He would hand them out when he was ready!

It was at that moment that Adorabella flitted up in a pretty yellow swimsuit, and

promptly helped herself to the biggest and best float! It was a green frog-shaped one, large enough for her to lie on. The other fairies protested, but she didn't care.

At last the fairies were all sorted and they darted off to jump into the water—squealing and gasping at how cold it was!

SPLOSH! SPLASH!

SPLOOOSH!

And while the fairies splashed and played, Adorabella drifted around on her float, bossily telling anyone off if they accidentally splashed her.

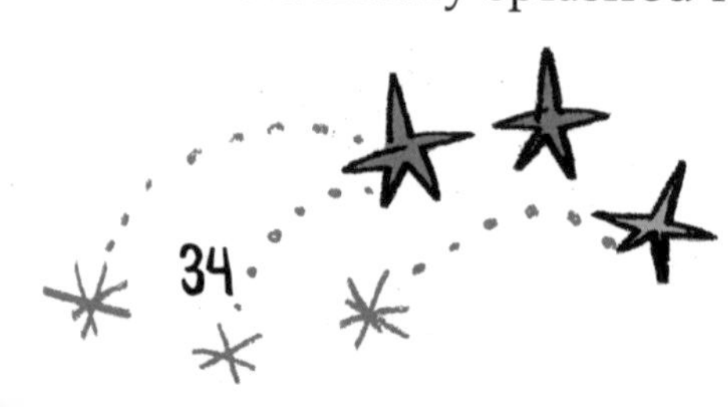

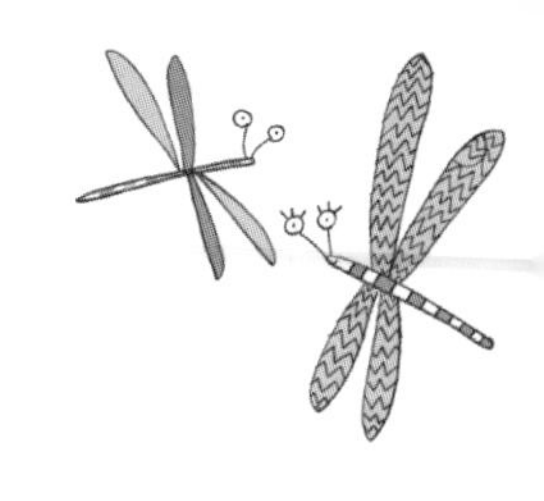

Chapter 4

SUPER SPLOSHY FUN

'Yahoooo!'

SPLOSH!

Some of the Water Fairies were doing star jumps and dive bombs off a lily pad in the middle of the pond, trying to make the biggest splash possible!

KER-SPLASH! SPLOOOOSH!

The rest of the Water Fairies, who were all brilliant swimmers, were taking it in turns to be lifeguards. They sat up in the trees looking out over the pond, with a float, a pair of binoculars, and a whistle.

Nixie and her friends were noisily splashing about in the pond, playing catch with a blow-up beach ball. Nixie had left her boots on the bank with Willow, who was sitting on the grass counting how many catches they did before someone dropped the ball.

Nixie chucked the wet ball at him.

SPLAT!

'Come and play!' she called.

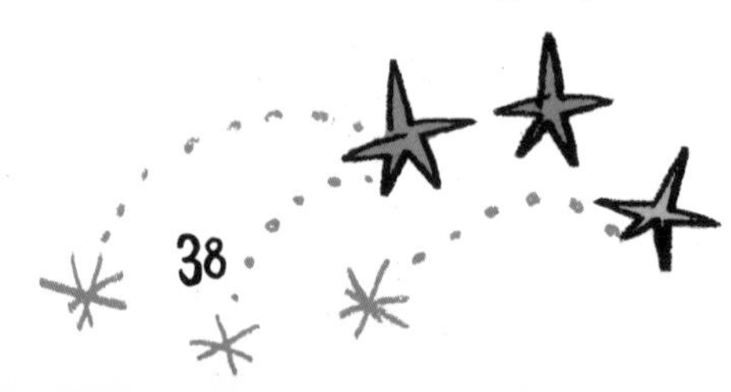

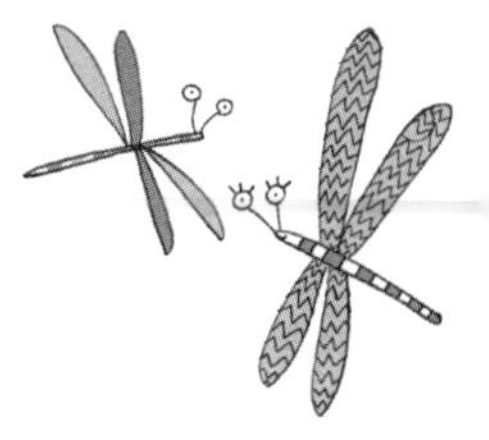

'It's too cold!' laughed Willow, throwing it back.

'Not when you get used to it,' said Briar. But Willow said he was happy to sit out and fetch the ball if it went out of the pond.

The Fairy Godmother, meanwhile, was trying to listen to music on her PeaPod. But fairies kept coming to ask her to blow up their armbands again, or to tighten their goggles. She was up and down off the sunlounger like a yo-yo!

'I don't mind just this once,' she repeated kindly, as she helped them all, 'but it is meant to be my day off, so can you please ask Buzby to help you next time.'

But there was already a long queue of fairies waiting for Buzby's help! He was frantically blowing up swim rings, fiddling with flippers, handing out pool toys, and making sure everyone had suncream on. He was hot and frazzled and his little furry body was smeared with lotion.

Lazing on the frog float, Adorabella drifted around getting in everyone's way until, accidentally on purpose, she floated into the middle of Nixie's game. Then, when Twist tried to throw the ball over her for

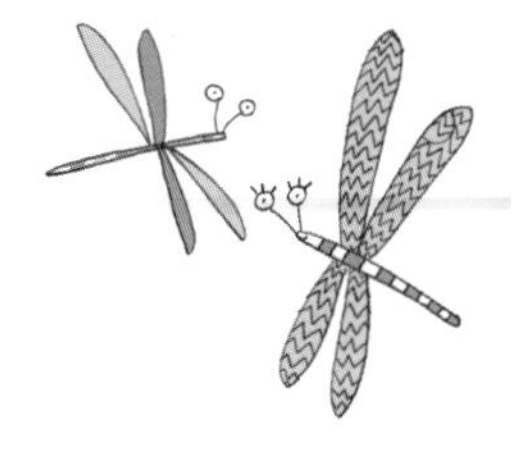

Fizz to catch, Adorabella reached up and snatched it out of the air!

'You nearly hit me!' she cried.

'No, I didn't!' said Twist. 'It was miles over your head!'

'Give us our ball back!' snapped Nixie.

'You can't expect to have all the pond to yourselves,' snipped Adorabella haughtily, still clutching the ball.

'GIVE IT BACK!' ordered Nixie.

'No!' gloated Adorabella.

Nixie grabbed hold of Adorabella's float and shook it violently.

'Don't!' cried Adorabella. 'I'll fall off!'

'Good!' retorted Nixie.

'Nixie, stop it!' squealed Adorabella,

loudly enough for the Fairy Godmother to hear—even with her PeaPod earphones in.

'Nixie!' said Tabitha Quicksilver wearily, without even opening her eyes. 'Whatever you're doing to annoy Adorabella—don't!'

'But she's got our ball!' cried Nixie.

'Play nicely!' called the Fairy Godmother, from under her sun umbrella.

Adorabella smirked and held the ball up like a trophy.

'Give it!' hissed Nixie.

'Can't make me!' taunted Adorabella.

I bet I can! thought Nixie.

And she darted out of the water and over to her boots, grabbed her wonky wand, and pointed it at Adorabella.

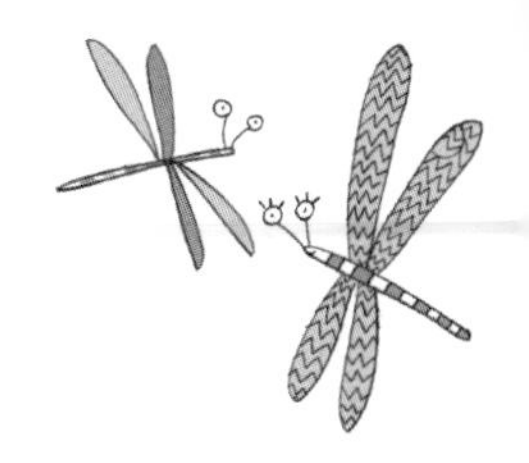

ZAP! WHOOOSH!

A shower of bright red fairy dust shot out of the wobbly star at the end and struck Adorabella's frog-shaped float.

FIZZ, SPLUTTER, SPLAT!

The float did a sort of hiccup and a wiggle and . . .

WHOOOMPH!

RIBBIT, RIBBIT!

It turned into a real frog! A huge slippery green one with great long legs, a big grinning mouth . . . and a fairy in a pretty yellow swimsuit on its back!

Chapter 5

ADORABELLA'S FROGGY-BACK RIDE!

RIBBIT, RIBBIT! BOING!

The frog leapt out of the Polished Pebble Pond and onto the bank—with Adorabella still clinging on!

'Help!' she cried, as it froggy-jumped across the grass in giant clumsy leaps.

'HELP!'

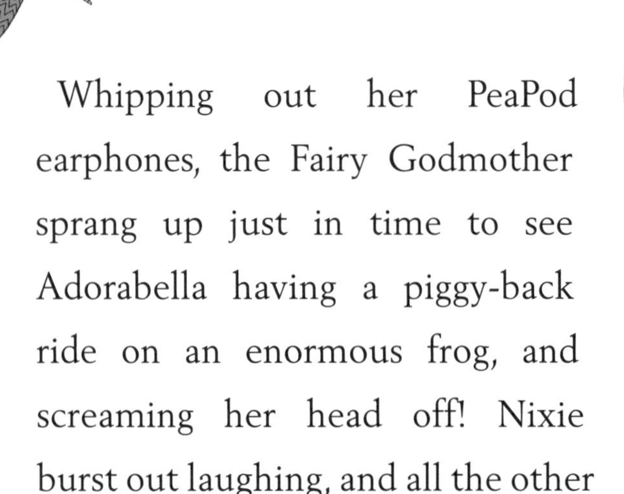

Whipping out her PeaPod earphones, the Fairy Godmother sprang up just in time to see Adorabella having a piggy-back ride on an enormous frog, and screaming her head off! Nixie burst out laughing, and all the other fairies gasped and giggled.

'Get off that frog immediately!' cried Tabitha Quicksilver.

'I can't!' wailed Adorabella.

'Just let go!' insisted the Fairy Godmother.

'Yes, just hop off!' laughed Nixie.

'It's going too fast!' howled Adorabella, as the frog took another huge jump.

BOING! RIBBIT!

Tabitha Quicksilver snatched up her wand and **TINGLE, TING!** a long ribbon of silver fairy dust streamed out towards Adorabella, twirled around her, and knotted itself into a bow. The Fairy Godmother gave her wand a gentle flick, and the fairy-dust ribbon plucked Adorabella off the frog and put her on the ground. Then **POUFF!** the ribbon disappeared in a shower of tiny sparkles.

The frog bounded happily away.

RIBBIT, LEAP, RIBBIT!

Adorabella clenched her fists and buzzed her wings angrily. 'You horrible hairy-fairy meany!' she bawled at Nixie.

'Adorabella!' scolded the Fairy Godmother. 'This is meant to be my day off! How is this helping?!'

Adorabella scowled at Nixie who glared back.

In order to keep the peace, the Fairy Godmother thought it would be a good idea to keep Nixie and Adorabella apart, so she let Adorabella lie on her sunlounger. She would take her brand new lilo onto the pond instead.

Adorabella slid gloatingly onto the

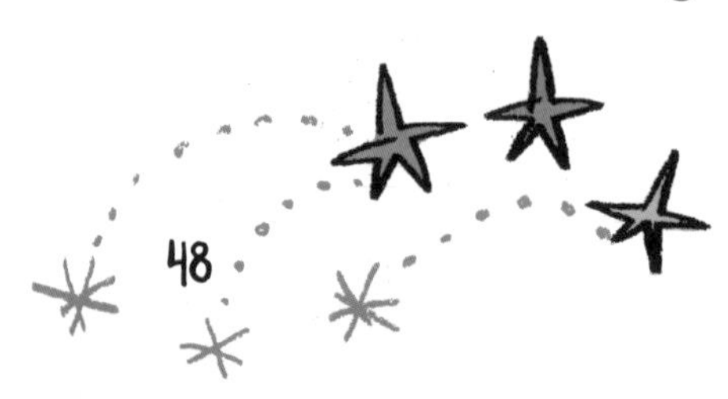

sunlounger. 'Thank you, Fairy Godmother,' she said sweetly. Nixie rolled her eyes.

The Fairy Godmother's new lilo was very snazzy. It was flower-shaped with purple petals, a pillow, and a cup holder for a drink. She hadn't even used it yet so it was lying limply on the floor. Buzby was far too busy to blow it up for her, so she asked Nixie instead. At least it would keep her out of mischief while the Fairy Godmother got herself a cool drink.

Nixie stared at the lilo in dismay. Not only was it very snazzy—it was also very large. It was going to take lots of puff to fill up all those petals! Her little wings drooped in despair.

Willow and Briar fluttered over to help.

'It's going to take for ever!' groaned Willow, watching Nixie blow furiously into the large lilo, her face going **redder** than her dress. The petals didn't seem to be filling up at all!

Nixie was tempted to use magic.

'But Nixie, your wonky wand hardly ever does what you want it to!' warned Willow.

'And anyway, we're not supposed to waste magic,' said Briar. 'Let's just take turns.'

While they blew up the lilo, the Fairy Godmother contentedly made herself a refreshing Lemon and Lime Fizzy Twizzler drink in a pretty plastic green tumbler. Then she added lots of crushed ice, a curly-whirly straw, and a turquoise cocktail umbrella.

When the lilo was finally blown up, the fairies put it on the pond and held it steady while the Fairy Godmother clambered on—which was a bit tricky because she was holding her Lemon and Lime Fizzy Twizzler at the same time. But finally she managed it, thanked the fairies for their help, and drifted off across the pond.

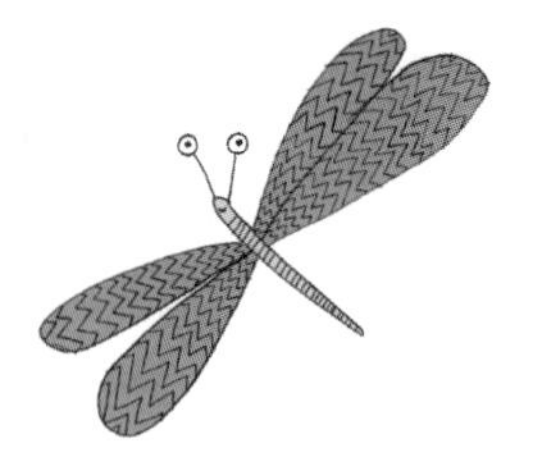

'Let's go back in the water and play catch,' said Briar.

'Can't we do something else?' asked Willow.

'Swimming?' suggested Nixie.

'No,' said Willow.

'I know, how about who can hold their breath underwater the longest?' said Nixie.

Willow shook his head. 'I don't want to go in the pond.'

'Why not?' asked Briar.

'I just don't,' shrugged Willow.

Nixie thought for a moment and then a broad grin lit up her grubby little face. 'Well, in that case,' she said, **'let's build a den!'**

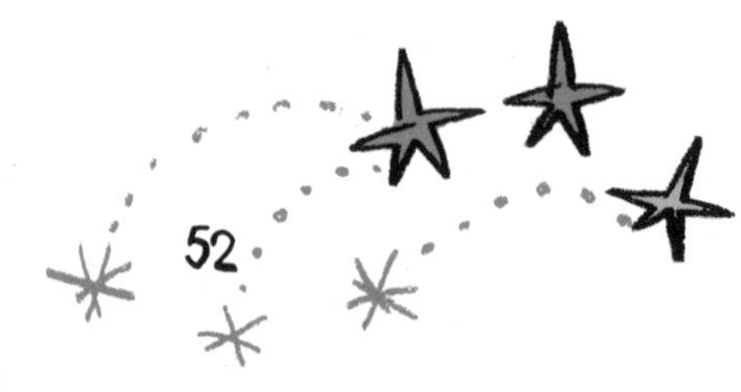

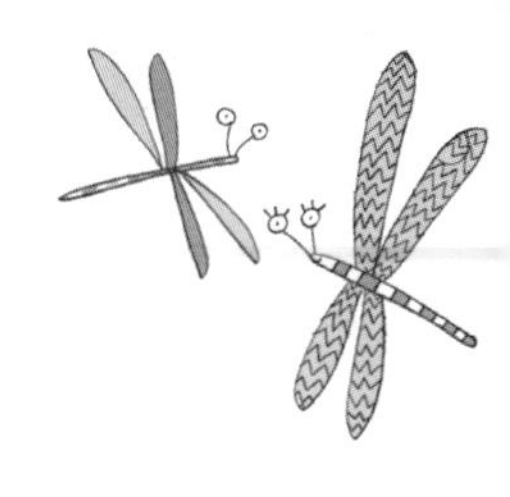

Chapter 6

BRILLIANTLY GRUBBY FUN!

Under the trees by the side of the pond, Nixie, Briar, and Willow scrabbled about looking for stuff to make a den.

'We want it big enough to stand up in,' said Willow.

'So we need some really long twigs,' said Nixie.

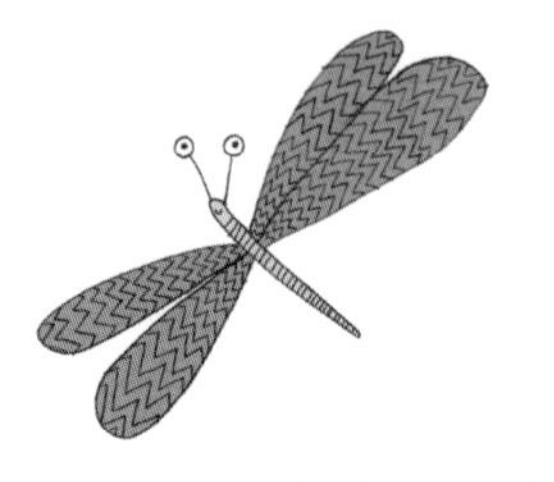

'How about this for a start?' cried Briar excitedly, dragging over a huge sturdy twig almost twice as tall as she was.

'Perfect!' cried Nixie. 'We need loads at least this big.' And she laid it on the ground so they could use it as a measure. They flitted about busily lugging twigs into a pile. Some were so big that it took all three fairies to lift them. It was a good job it was cool in the shade.

'How many are we going to need?' asked Briar breathlessly, as she struggled with a really heavy one.

'Well, the den's got to be **enormous**,' replied Nixie, 'so probably about a hundred?'

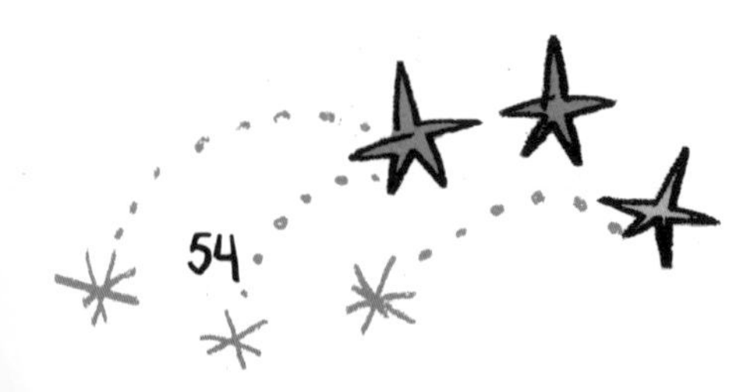

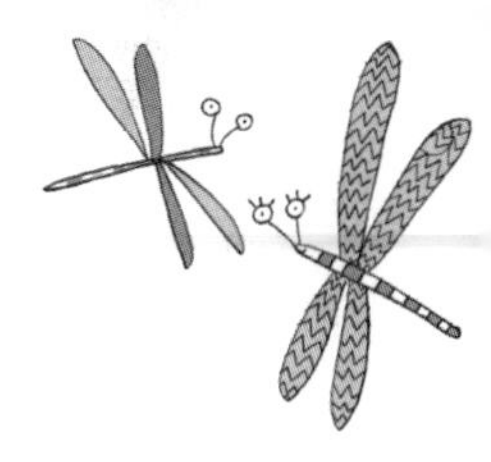

'A hundred!' exclaimed Briar.

Willow glanced at Nixie. 'She's joking,' he laughed. Nixie grinned mischievously.

Willow eyed the mound of twigs.

'Actually, that's probably enough.'

'But how are we actually going to build the den?' asked Briar.

'We could get all the twigs in a circle and lean them all together at the top, like a wigwam?' suggested Willow.

'And we should tie them together,' said Nixie. 'It'll make it stronger.'

'Good idea,' said Willow, picking up his rucksack. 'I've got some wool in here somewhere.' He rummaged through his collection of seeds, dried stalks, grass

leaves, empty nutshells, and other handy stuff until, after lots of searching, he found it. Then the three friends started hauling the twigs upright, one by one, and leaning them together at the top.

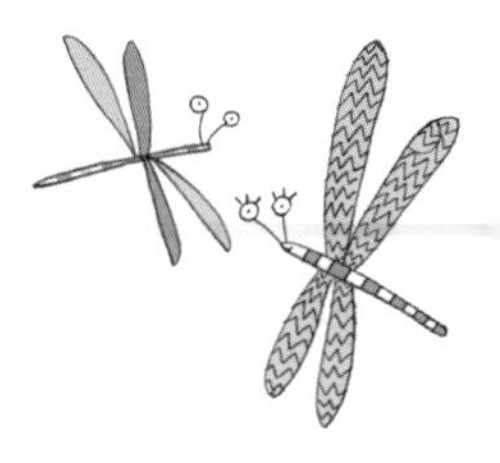

'Leave a gap for a doorway,' reminded Nixie.

It was messy work but the den was starting to take shape. And as the pile of twigs got smaller and smaller, the three fairies got grubbier and grubbier. It was **brilliant!**

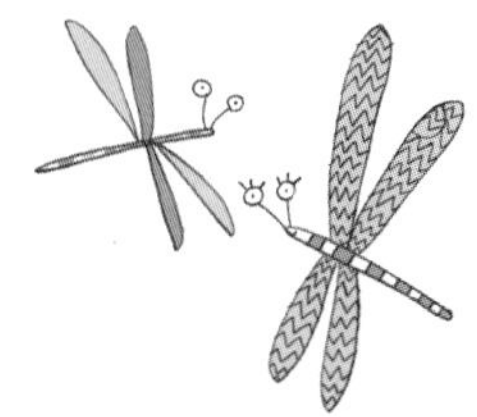

In the pond, the rest of the fairies were all splashing around happily. But poor Buzby was still on the bank surrounded by a whole heap of broken swimming stuff.

He was carefully making piles of things that could be mended and things that needed throwing away. There was a stack of

broken foam floats, some goggles, a couple of armbands, and he was just checking a swimming ring. He thought it had a hole in it, so he'd blown it up and now he was squeezing it and listening carefully to see if he could hear any hissing as the air escaped.

Suddenly . . .

RIBBIT, RIBBIT!

BOING!

Buzby looked up to see the frog had come back, and it was leaping cheerfully across the grass, heading straight towards him! Buzby's antennae waggled in alarm and

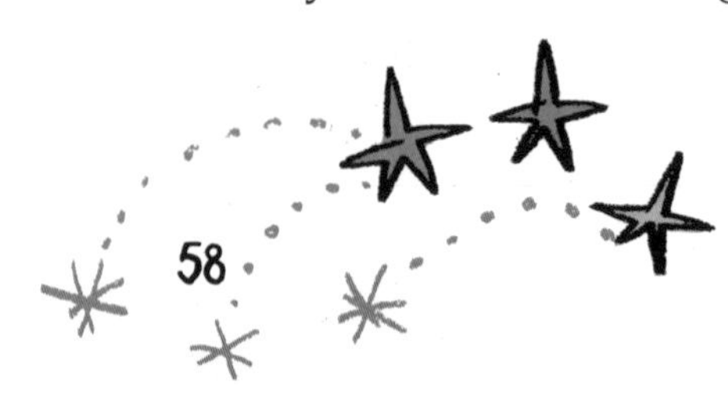

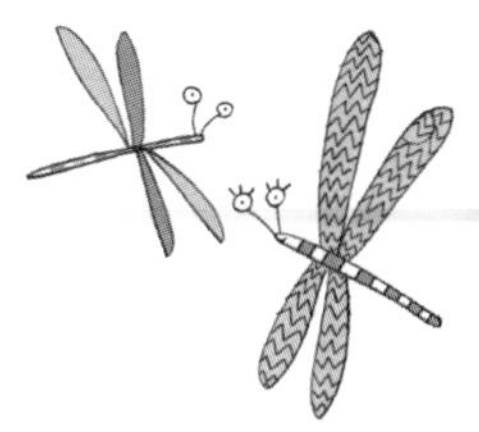

he **BUZZED** loudly. But the frog paid no attention, took a big jump, and almost landed on top of Buzby!

The little bee darted to one side, but the frog's back leg got caught up in the swim ring he was mending. Buzby let go, but the frog panicked and took off round the pond—with the ring still round its leg! Buzby chased after it, beating his little wings furiously to keep up.

RIBBIT, RIBBIT!

BUZZ, BUZZ!

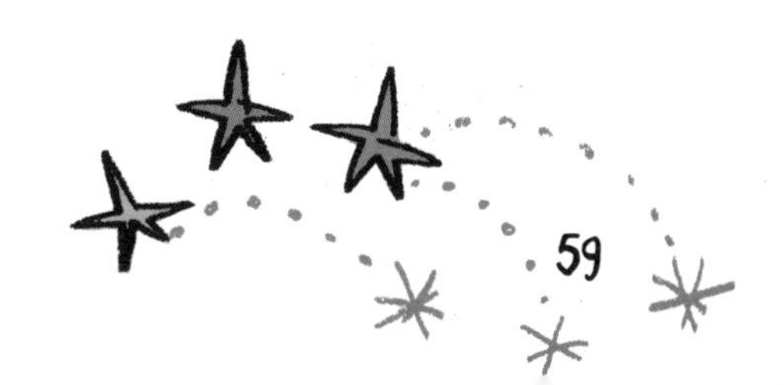

Chapter 7

A SOFT POP AND A LOUD HISS

Meanwhile, the Fairy Godmother was drifting around the pond on her lilo, and sipping her Lemon and Lime Fizzy Twizzler through the **curly-whirly** straw.

She had closed her eyes and was trying to relax, but it was a bit difficult with the deafening hubbub and total pandemonium

going on all around her!

Fairies shrieked and squealed, sploshed and splashed, jumped and dived, and hurled foam floats around in the air, whacking them down on the water with a mighty

KER-SPLOSH!

Fizz, Fidget, and Twist were playing 'piggy in the middle' with the beach ball. Fizz hurled the ball up over Twist for Fidget to catch. But it was too high and it sailed past Fidget and bumped the Fairy Godmother on the elbow. She nearly dropped her Lemon and Lime Fizzy Twizzler cocktail in the pond!

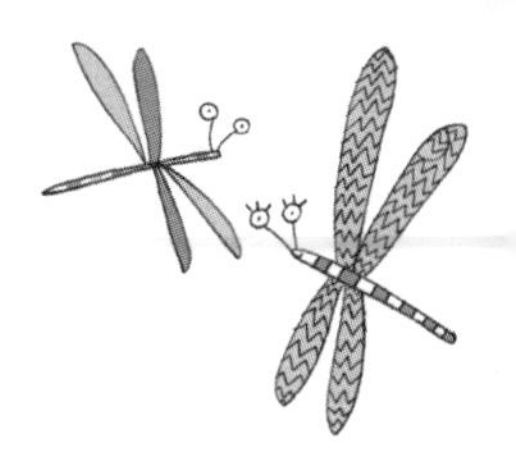

'I'm sorry!' cried Fizz.

'Never mind,' sighed the Fairy Godmother, tossing the ball back. 'No harm done.'

But she decided to let her flower lilo drift to the edge of the pond—well out of the way of the boisterous fairies. She headed towards the shade of the trees, looking forward to a little peace and quiet.

'This is bliss!' she sighed floating along, sunlight dappling through the leaves. And soon, lulled by the gentle rocking of the lilo on the water, she dozed off.

Under the trees nearby, Nixie, Willow, and Briar were placing the last few twigs on their den and tying them up, when . . .

RIBBIT, RIBBIT, RIBBIT!

BUZZ, BUZZ, BUZZ!

The frog, still with its back leg caught in the deflated swimming ring, was leaping towards them. Buzby was in hot pursuit!

'Oi! Watch out!' yelled Nixie, but . . .

CRASH! WALLOP!

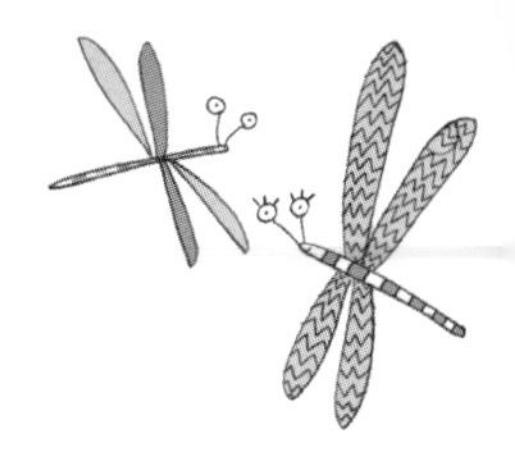

the frog blundered slap-bang into the den—and demolished it.

'You stupid frog!' bawled Nixie.

But the frog was already leaping away, with the rubber ring flapping and flopping as it hopped. By now Buzby was quite out of breath and utterly exhausted, so he gave up the chase and plonked himself down on the ground, panting and puffing.

The fairies gazed at the jumbled heap of twigs in dismay.

'All that work!' moaned Briar.

'And we'd nearly finished it,' groaned Willow.

'Come on,' said Nixie crossly, 'we'll just have to start again!'

Angrily, she picked up one of the large twigs and, without looking behind her, swung it carelessly round.

There was a soft POP! . . . a loud HISS! and an even louder GASP from the Fairy Godmother, who had woken with a start!

The end of Nixie's twig had stabbed into her snazzy new lilo—and popped it!

HISSSS . . .

WHOOOSH!

The flower float shot off like a balloon does when you blow it up and let it go—with the Fairy Godmother still lying

on top of it, clutching her Lemon and Lime Fizzy Twizzler cocktail!

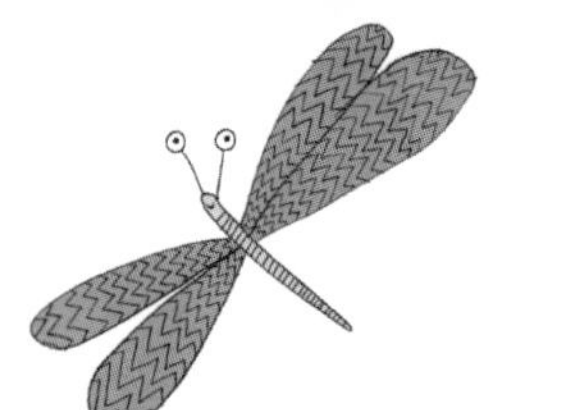

The lilo zigzagged crazily around the pond, taking Tabitha Quicksilver with it! As it whizzed over the surface, fairies squealed and darted out of the way, or dived under the water. The lilo hurtled towards the bank, where it hit a tree—BOING, bounced harmlessly off, and rocketed back across the pond, almost knocking over Buzby. Then it spun round and whooshed towards Adorabella, who screamed and ducked just in time.

'Bumblebees' bottoms!' gasped Nixie.

Chapter 8

FIZZY TWIZZLER TROUBLE!

At last, when it was completely empty of air, the flower lilo skidded up the bank and flopped limply onto the grass. The Fairy Godmother landed on top of it with a **BUMP!** She was still clutching her Lemon and Lime Fizzy Twizzler—and she hadn't spilled a drop.

With a good deal of dignity she put the tumbler down and fluttered over to Nixie.

Everyone watched anxiously, except Adorabella who smirked. Nixie was going to be in big, big trouble.

Nixie's little black wings drooped miserably. 'I'm sorry,' she said. 'It was an accident.'

'It was careless!' corrected the Fairy Godmother sharply. 'And you really must learn to be more careful. So now you can mend it.'

Nixie sighed, but she didn't argue.

Tabitha Quicksilver suddenly felt rather dizzy.

'I think I need a little lie-down,' she said

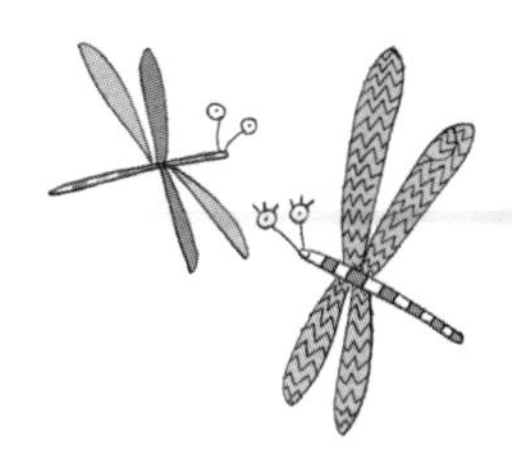

weakly, and fluttered off giddily to tell Adorabella she wanted the sunlounger back. Reluctantly Adorabella slid off it, glowering at Nixie.

Nixie examined the lilo carefully and soon found the hole.

'It just needs a little patch,' she said confidently.

Willow dug around in his rucksack.

'How about this?' he said, handing Nixie a small leaf.

'Brilliant! Have you got any glue?'

Willow shook his head.

'Haven't you got some in your workshop?' asked Briar.

'I'm not going all the way home just to get

a dollop of glue!' said Nixie, reaching into her boot for her wand.

Willow and Briar exchanged nervous looks.

'It's only a teeny-tiny little hole—so it'll only need a teeny-tiny little bit of magic. It'll be fine,' said Nixie.

But her naughty wand had other ideas, and when Nixie pointed it at the lilo . . .

ZAP, FIZZ! WHOOOOOOSH!

A stream of bright red fairy dust gushed out, deliberately missed the lilo and hit the

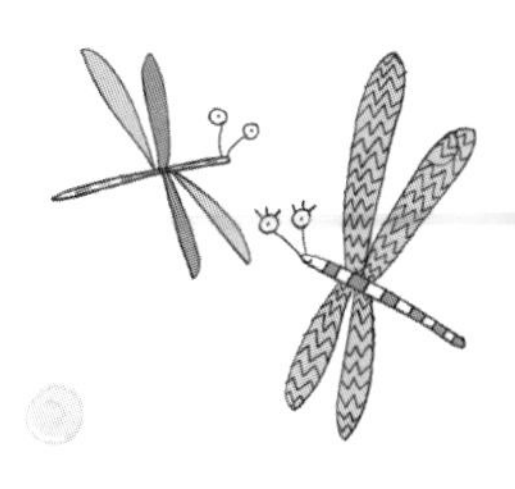

Lemon and Lime Fizzy Twizzler drink instead!

'Oh no!' gasped Nixie.

The tumbler trembled violently, and promptly doubled in size, and then again . . . and again—until it was as big as Nixie, and the curly-whirly straw was much taller than even the Fairy Godmother!

FIZZLE-FIZZLE-FIZZ!

The drink inside bubbled furiously and then, WHOOOOSH! a foaming fountain of froth burst out of the giant straw like an exploding volcano.

TWIZZLE-TWIZZLE-WHIZZ!

The curly-whirly straw whirled crazily round and round, plastering everyone with foaming Lemon and Lime Fizzy Twizzler!

SPLUTTER, SPLATTER, SPLOOSH!

The Fairy Godmother had just about had enough!

'OH, FOR GOODNESS' SAKE!' she snapped, snatching up her sparkly silver wand.

TING! A-TING, TING! Fairy dust

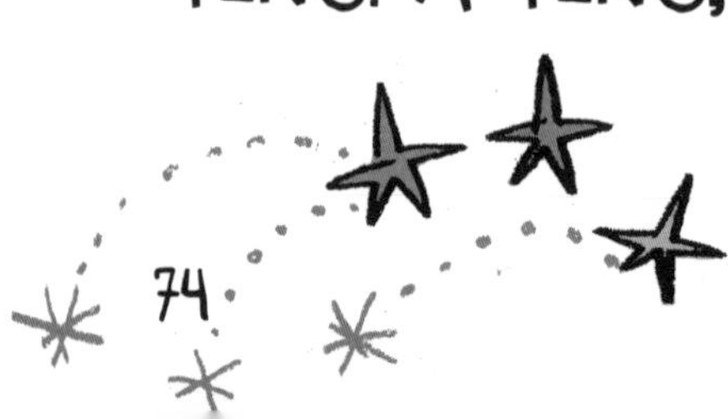

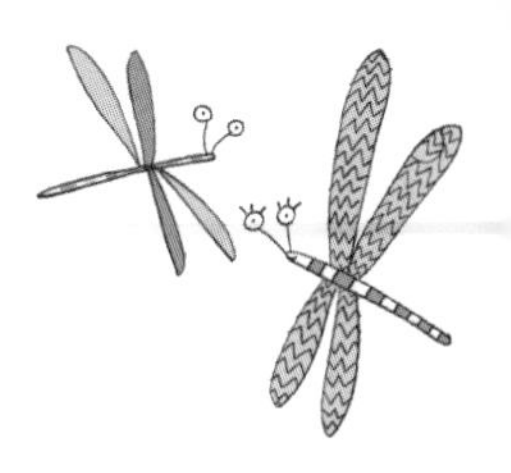

shot out and struck the giant tumbler so hard it almost toppled over. But instead it did an almighty WRIGGLE and a massive WIBBLE-WOBBLE and then WHEEEEEEEE! went back to its proper size. The curly-whirly straw stopped spinning, shrank back to normal, and gave an embarrassed little burp.

Finally, the huge frothy mound of bubbles burst harmlessly in the air.

POP-POPATY-POP-a-POP!

'You did that on purpose,' Nixie yelled at her mischievous wand, shaking it so crossly the wonky red star nearly fell off.

Tabitha Quicksilver was almost lost for words.

'Nixie, just . . . just . . .' she stammered. 'Just . . . go and play somewhere else, and please try to keep out of trouble!'

So, while the other fairies went back to their splashy fun in the pond, Nixie stomped off to the den. Willow and Briar followed her.

'Nixie's dreadful, isn't she?' said Adorabella smugly to Tabitha Quicksilver. The Fairy Godmother silenced her with a look and a raised eyebrow.

Chapter 9

NIXIE'S WET AND WACKY INVENTION!

Briar and Willow started building the den again, but Nixie flopped down grumpily on a tree root and glowered.

'Give us a hand, Nixie!' said Briar.

'I'm not in the mood,' she replied, crabbily.

'You shouldn't have used your wand!'

said Willow.

'It wasn't all your fault,' added Briar, soothingly.

'It wasn't my fault at all!' said Nixie, hotly. 'It was my **stupid wonky wand!**'

'Let's find something else fun to do,' said Briar.

She's right, thought Nixie, there's no point wasting time being miserable when you can be having fun!

So they hunted around for something interesting to play with. Nixie found a big clump of buttercups with their bright yellow waxy petals—and that gave her an idea for some **wacky water fun!**

She told Briar and Willow to fetch the

watering can and a wheelbarrow. Then, while they were gone, she set about picking up lots and lots of fallen petals from the buttercup patch.

By the time her friends got back, she had a huge pile.

'What are we going to do with all those?' asked Briar.

'Guess!' said Nixie, her green eyes glittering with glee.

Willow and Briar looked at each other and shrugged. They had no idea.

'Hold that,' ordered Nixie, handing Briar a

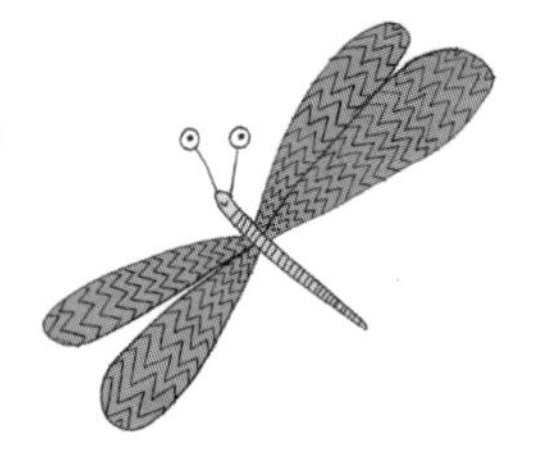

petal. 'Both hands. Now bend up the sides like a cup—and don't let go!' Picking up the watering can, she half-filled the yellow petal with water.

'Willow, quick! Grab some wool and tie it up. Really tight so the water can't spill out.'

It was a bit tricky and it took all three of them to do it—but they finally managed it.

'Watch this!' said Nixie taking the water-filled petal from Briar.

Sticking her tongue out of her mouth in concentration, she took aim . . . and hurled the flower at a nearby tree trunk with all her fairy might!

Wheeee!

SPLAT!

Bang on target, it smacked against the trunk and BURST! Water showered everywhere!

SPLOSH!

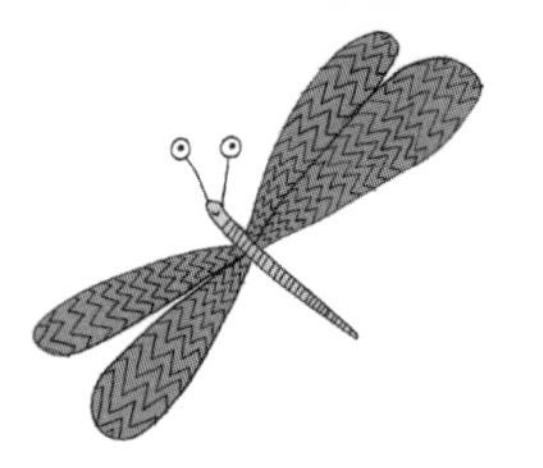

Nixie had invented the Buttercup Water Bomb!

'YAHOO!' she yelled.

'Nixie, you are a genius!' cried Willow.

Nixie folded her arms. 'We are going to have a massive water bomb fight with absolutely everybody!' she announced.

'We're going to need loads,' warned Willow.

'Loads and loads,' said Briar.

'Loads and loads and LOADS!' laughed Nixie gleefully.

They spent the next hour or so making water bombs and piling them carefully into the wheelbarrow. At first they struggled to tie them tightly enough so that they didn't

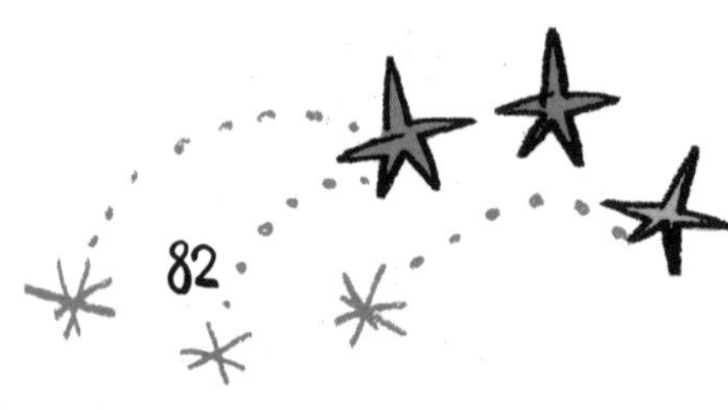

leak. But after they'd done a few they got the hang of it.

The pile of petals by the side of the tree got smaller and the mound of buttercup bombs got bigger—until the barrow was completely full.

Nixie grabbed the handles of the wheelbarrow. 'Let's go!' she shouted excitedly. 'It's time for a **WET AND WACKY WATER BOMB BATTLE** in the pond!'

'Bagsie I'm on your side!' said Briar. She knew what a good thrower Nixie was.

'You're both on my team!' grinned Nixie, and she was just about to say who else she wanted, but Willow announced he

wanted to stay behind and build the den instead.

'What?' cried Nixie, stopping the wheelbarrow in surprise.

'Why?' asked Briar.

Willow shrugged. 'I don't like going in the pond.'

'But the pond is the best place ever on a boiling hot day like today!' exclaimed Nixie.

'It's a bit cold to start with but you soon get used to it,' said Briar.

'It's fine if you just jump in!' nodded Nixie.

'I can't "just jump in",' said Willow sadly. 'I can't swim.'

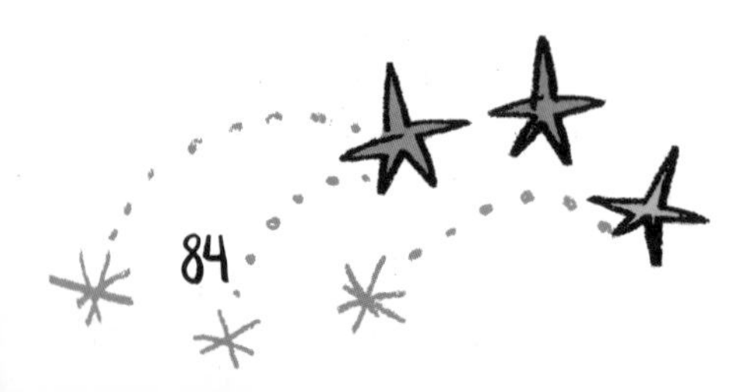

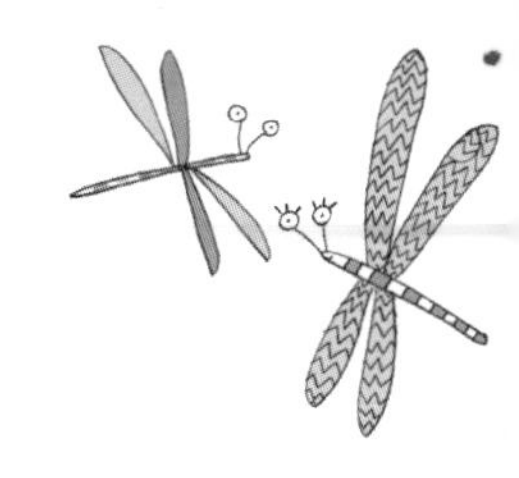

Chapter 10

FABULOUS FISHY IDEA!

Willow's friends looked at each other. They had no idea that Willow couldn't swim. Nixie burst out laughing!

'Is that all?' she said. 'We'll teach you to swim!' And, grabbing Willow's hand she tried to drag him down to the pond.

But Willow pulled his hand away.

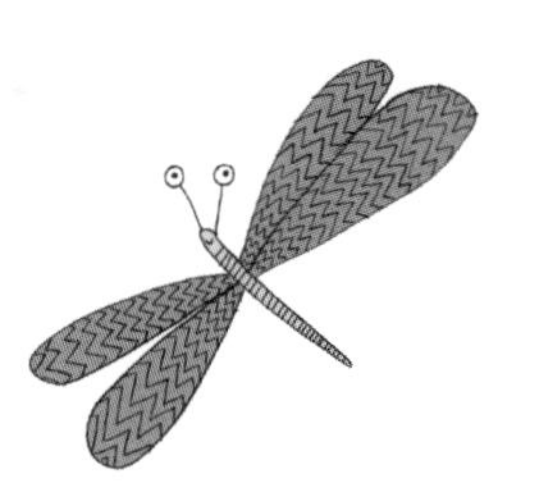

'NO! DON'T!' he yelled. 'I don't want to.'

'Why not?' asked Briar.

'I'm scared of the water.'

He looked like he was about to cry, so

Nixie gave him a big hug and said, 'It's all right, Willow. There's nothing to be frightened of, honest!'

'That's easy for you to say,' said Willow. 'You can swim.'

'But I didn't used to be able to. I was always too scared to take my feet off the bottom until I started using armbands.'

But Willow had tried armbands and he didn't like them. 'They're too tight and they pinch,' he said.

'I hate getting water on my face and it scares me when it goes up my nose,' said Briar, 'so I use a swimming ring.'

'I don't want one of those. I'm scared I'll slip out,' said Willow.

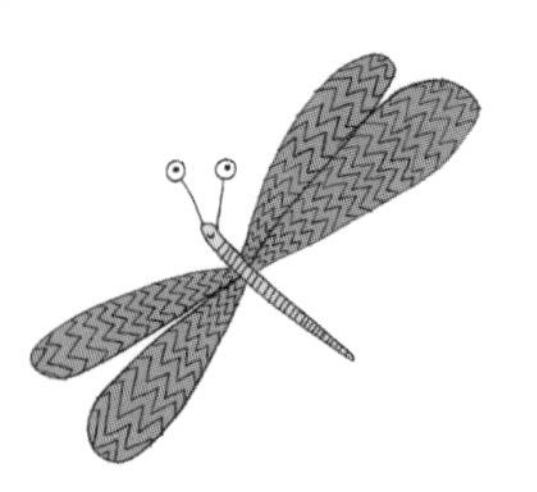

'What about a float?' suggested Briar.

'I don't like them because you have to hold onto them and I'm scared I'll let go,' said Willow.

Hmmm, thought Nixie, *teaching Willow to swim might be tricky. Unless I can invent something to help.*

'Just give me a minute to think,' she said, sitting down on the floor with her legs crossed and her chin in her hands.

She had to come up with something he wouldn't need to hold onto, that wasn't too tight, but not so loose that he'd worry about it falling off.

She looked across at the other fairies playing in the pond—maybe something

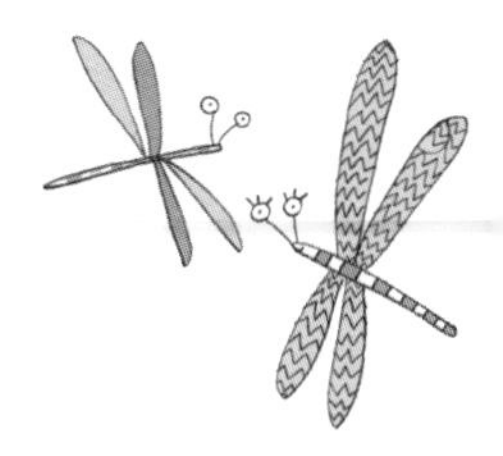

would give her an idea. She watched the Water Fairies darting around in the water, and diving right under. *Maybe we could ask one of them to help?* she thought, *they can all swim like fishes.*

And then a brilliant idea hit her!

'Fishes! That's it!' she cried. 'Willow, I know how you can swim like a fish—I'll give you a fin!'

'Noooo!' cried Willow, thinking Nixie was going to use magic on him and he'd either grow a fin, or worse still, turn into a goldfish!

'Nixie! Don't even think about using your wonky wand on Willow!' warned Briar.

'I'm not going to!' laughed Nixie. 'I'm going to *make* him a fin!'

the big worktable in the middle of the room and drew the shape of a fin on it with a pencil. Then, going over to the tools she kept hanging on nails all along one wall, she took down her saw.

Since she couldn't safely hold the float in one hand and saw it with the other, she clamped the float tightly in the vice she kept mounted on the workbench. Then she began to saw along the pencil lines. The foam made a funny noise as she cut through it!

SAW, SAW, SAW.

SQUEAK, SQUEAK, SQUEAK!

When she'd finished sawing, she got her penknife and carefully cut two holes in the float. Then she looked through the boxes of odds and ends under her workbench for something to make a harness. There was a reel of cobweb thread—but she thought that would be too thin and uncomfortable.

Then she found an old belt.

That'll do the job! She threaded it through the holes.

'Perfect!' she announced and, picking up the float, she fluttered back to the pond and proudly presented it to Willow.

He gave the fin a funny look, but he trusted Nixie's inventions. So Briar held the float steady while Nixie slipped the

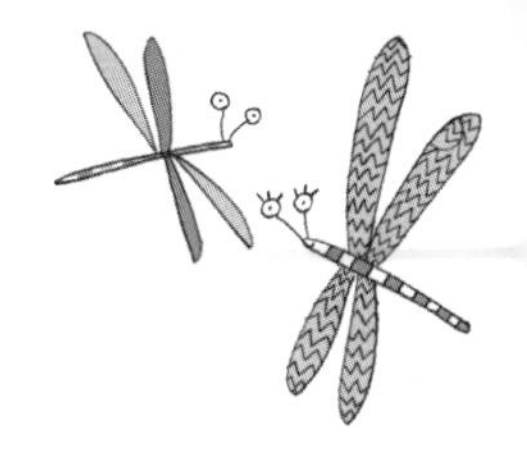

belt round Willow's tummy and buckled it firmly. The float stuck up from Willow's back like a fin! He looked like a fish fairy!

'Ready?' asked Nixie.

Willow nodded nervously.

'Hold tight then,' she said as she and Briar held his hands and slid into the pond. Then, slowly, they swam off, towing Willow between them.

'Don't go too deep,' said Willow anxiously.

'We'll stay by the edge,' promised Briar.

'If you don't like it you can just stand up,' said Nixie.

The fin float worked brilliantly, and made Willow feel much braver.

'Look at me! **I'm floating!**' he cried

excitedly, happily kicking his legs as they swam round and round the pond. Then, after a while, he let go of Nixie and Briar and started doing a splashy sort of doggy paddle—all on his own.

Meanwhile, Adorabella was swimming

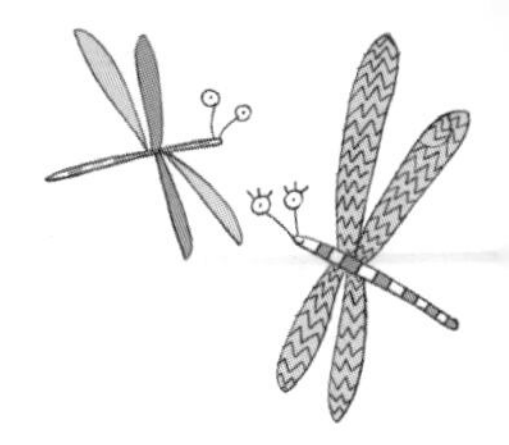

daintily around trying not to get splashed by Fizz and Fidget who were playing tag with Twist. When she saw Willow's float, she swam up to him nosily. 'What's that supposed to be?' she demanded.

'It's a fin,' snapped Nixie.

'No it's not, it's a tatty old float.' And turning back to Willow, she added, 'You look ridiculous!'

'Don't be so mean,' said Briar.

'He can't help it if he can't swim,' said Nixie.

'Can't you even swim?!' snorted Adorabella, laughing at Willow.

Willow glared at her.

'Just ignore her,' said Briar.

But Nixie was furious. She crossed her arms and glared at Adorabella. 'Say sorry right now, or I'll get my wand and give you a fish fin too . . . and a fishy tail, to match your silly fish-face!'

'You wouldn't fairy dare!' gloated Adorabella, 'not with the Fairy Godmother sitting over there.'

Nixie glanced over to where Tabitha Quicksilver was lying on her lounger, reading a book.

Adorabella was right; she didn't dare. Smugly, Adorabella swam off.

'I'm so going to get you back for that!' seethed Nixie.

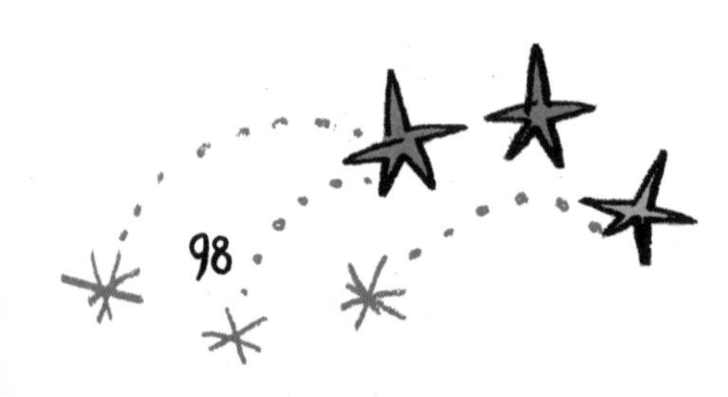

Chapter 12

BRILLIANT WATER BOMB BATTLE!

Willow was upset—but not with Adorabella, with Nixie! He didn't want anyone to know he couldn't swim.

'But that's daft,' said Nixie. 'Fidget can't swim at all! That's why she wears armbands!'

'Everyone's got something they can't do,' said Briar. 'I can't do cartwheels.'

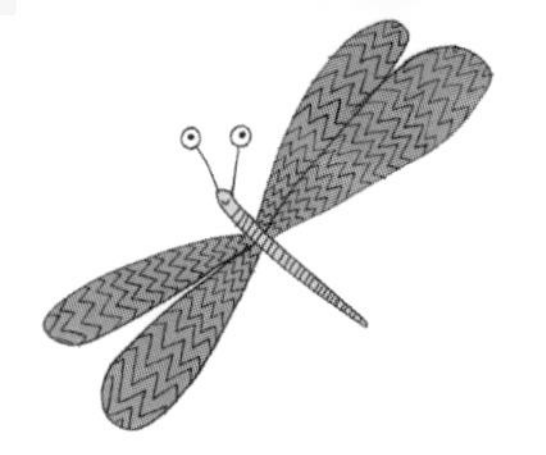

'And you should see me trying to do a bottom-sit on the trampoline! I'm rubbish!' laughed Nixie. 'And anyway, you can swim—in your fin float!' she pointed out.

Willow grinned.

Nixie's eyes lit up gleefully. 'Come on,' she said, 'let's get the water bombs!'

So they darted over to the wheelbarrow and pushed it over to the pond.

Nixie took a big breath and bellowed, **'WHO WANTS A WATER BOMB FIGHT!?'**

Whooping and squealing, the fairies rushed over, grabbed the water bombs, and started hurling them at each other! Buttercup petals whizzed across the pool

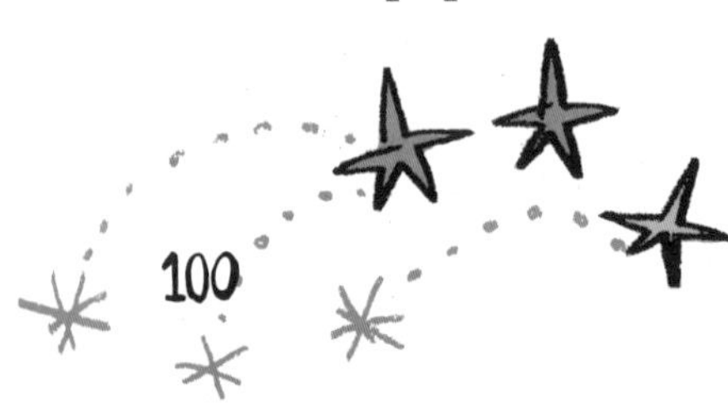

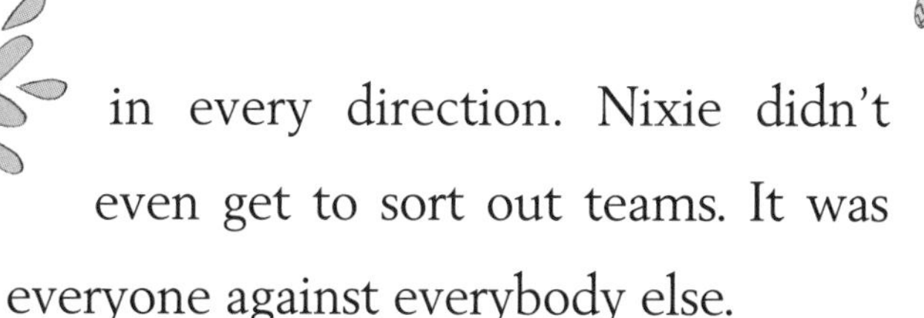

in every direction. Nixie didn't even get to sort out teams. It was everyone against everybody else.

SPLASH, SPLATTER!
KA-SPLOOOOSH!

Nixie threw one at Willow—but he managed to catch it, and promptly chucked it straight back at her!

She squealed, held her nose, and ducked under the water.

SPLOOOOOSH!

The flower bomb burst on the surface. 'Missed!' yelled Nixie triumphantly as she bobbed up again, but . . .

SPLOSH!

A water bomb splattered into her arm!

'Gotcha!' cried Fidget.

'I'll get you for that!' laughed Nixie, dashing off to get her own back.

Briar was sheltering behind a water lily, while Fizz and Twist lobbed water bombs at her.

Wheeee . . .

'Na na nana nah! Can't get me-e!' gloated Briar as the water bombs sailed past her and exploded near the Water Fairies who all shrieked and dived underwater.

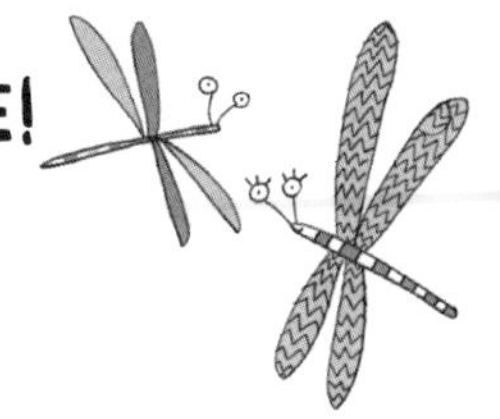

SPLAT! SPLATTER, SPLOSH!

On her sunlounger, Tabitha Quicksilver gave up trying to read and watched the fairies' super soggy water battle instead. It was hilarious!

Every single fairy had joined in—except, guess who? Adorabella. She was livid.

'You can't take over the whole pond!' she screeched at Nixie.

'Why not? Everyone's playing!' pointed out Nixie.

'I'm not!'

'Oh yes, you are!' said Nixie, immediately chucking a water bomb straight at her.

WHEEEEE!

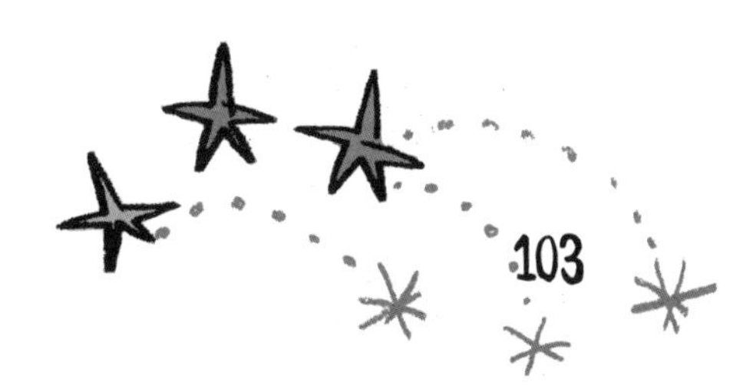

the Fairy Godmother.

Nixie grinned cheekily. 'NO! I threw it at her,' she said pointing at Adorabella, 'but she ducked and it hit you! So it's all her fault!'

'But I wasn't even playing!' wailed Adorabella.

'Yes you were!' retorted Nixie.

'FAIRIES! Please!' cried the Fairy Godmother. 'That's quite enough! Now, I think it would be a good idea for everyone to get out of the pond for a little while and calm down.'

Everybody groaned, until the Fairy Godmother smiled and added, 'And I'll make everyone an ice cream—in any flavour you like!'

Chapter 13

ADORABELLA'S ICE-SCREAM!

There was a lot of splashing as the fairies scrambled out of the pond and raced over to the Fairy Godmother to get their ice creams.

Adorabella made sure she was first in the queue and instantly asked for a triple chocolate cone with chocolate chips,

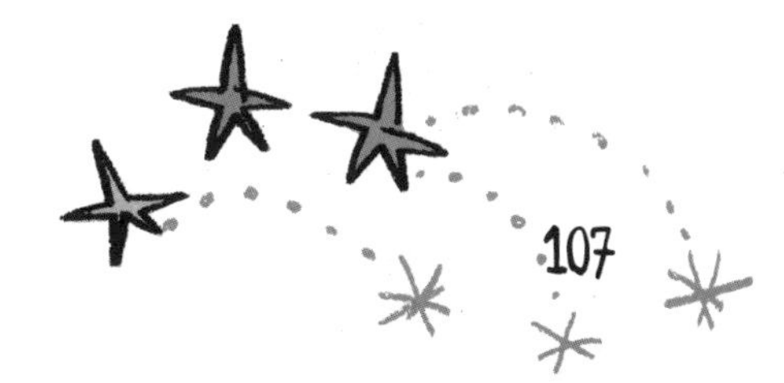

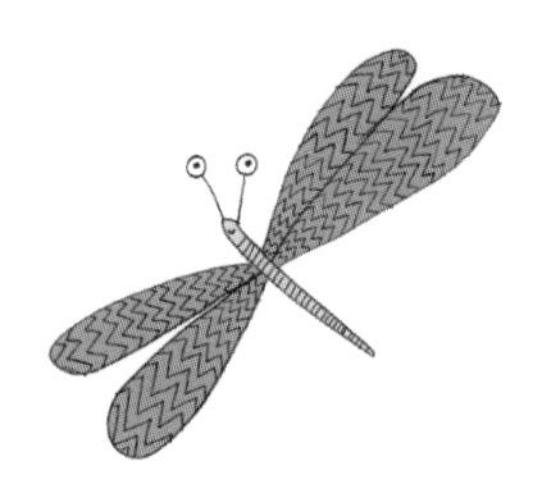

chocolate sauce, and a chocolate stick in each scoop!

TING-A-TING! went the Fairy Godmother's wand and she handed Adorabella an enormous ice cream!

Briar wanted strawberry and vanilla with raspberry sauce. **TING!**

Willow had butterscotch topped with maple syrup and nuts. **TINGLE, TING!**

When it was Nixie's turn she asked for cookies and cream with raspberries and candy sprinkles on top. **TING!** went the Fairy Godmother's wand.

'No, wait,' said Nixie, 'I've changed my mind . . . I want a double-mint choc-chip in a chocolate cornet.'

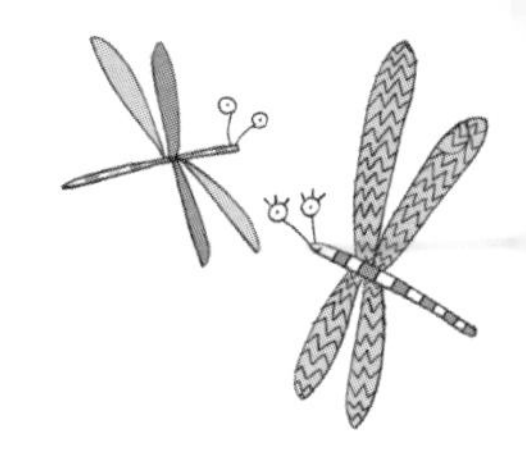

The Fairy Godmother sighed, but she changed Nixie's ice cream. **TING-A-TINGLE!**

'Actually, I think I want blueberry bubble gum,' said Nixie.

The Fairy Godmother rolled her eyes. 'In a chocolate cornet?'

'Yes. No! In a plain one.'

Tabitha Quicksilver raised her wand again.

'No, wait!' cried Nixie. 'Can I have white chocolate with cranberries and chocolate chips? No, hang on, toffee caramel with fudge sauce . . .'

'Are you sure that's what you want?' asked Tabitha Quicksilver.

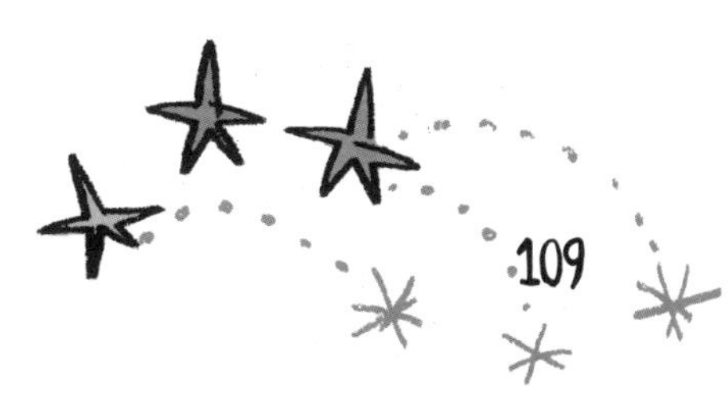

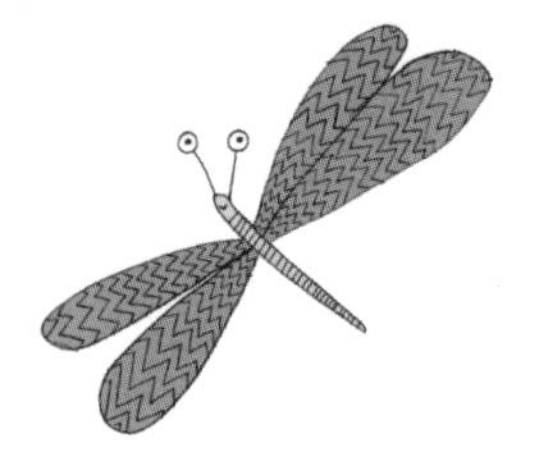

'Um . . . no,' said Nixie anxiously. It was just too hard to choose!

So the Fairy Godmother decided for her. TING-A-TING! She handed Nixie a huge cone—half chocolate and half plain—with a scoopful of every single flavour she'd asked for, all smothered in fudge sauce and candy sprinkles.

'Perfect!' beamed Nixie greedily, taking a massive slurp.

Soon all the fairies were sitting round on the grass, drying their wings in the warm sunshine and licking ice creams. Even Buzby had one—vanilla and honeycomb with honey drizzle.

Tabitha Quicksilver kicked off her shoes

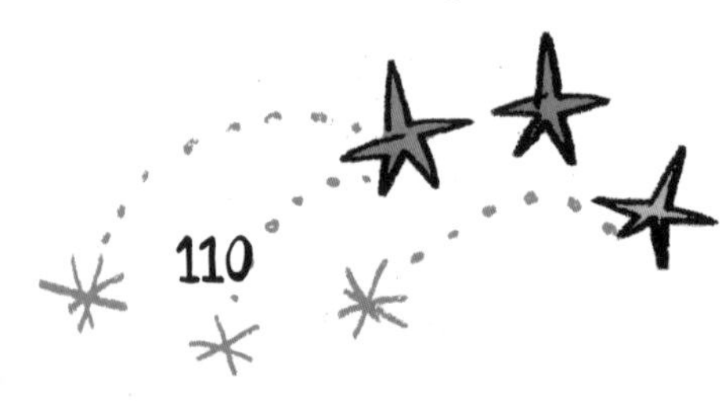

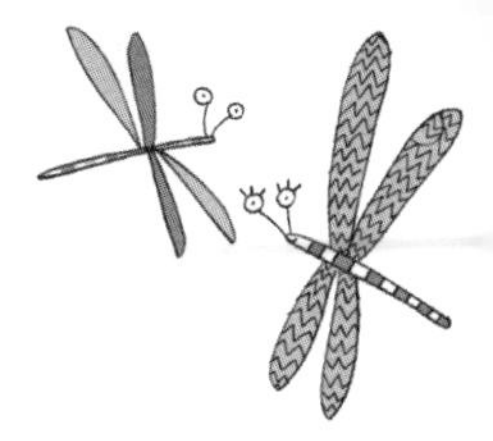

and sank wearily onto the sunlounger. Her day off had been even more exhausting than a normal day! But at last, she could relax. She closed her eyes and sighed contentedly.

But suddenly, there was a loud **GASP!** And a piercing **SCREAM!**

It was Adorabella.

She'd been bragging about what a brilliant swimmer she was. 'Not like some people,' she had added, smirking at Willow.

Briar had rolled her eyes and Willow had glared. But, remembering how horrible Adorabella had been to her friend earlier, Nixie decided it was time to get revenge.

So Nixie had crept over to get her wand

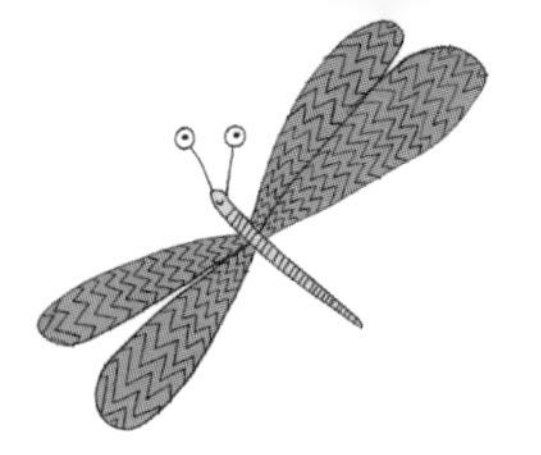

and, while Adorabella was busily eating her ice cream, she had silently tiptoed up behind, pointed her wonky wand at Adorabella's ice cream, and given it a sneaky flick!

And this time, for once, her mischievous wand had done exactly what she wanted!

ZAP! FIZZZZZ! A stream of tiny red sparkles had whizzed over and struck the ice cream cone smack on target. And Adorabella's delicious triple chocolate ice cream with chocolate chips, chocolate

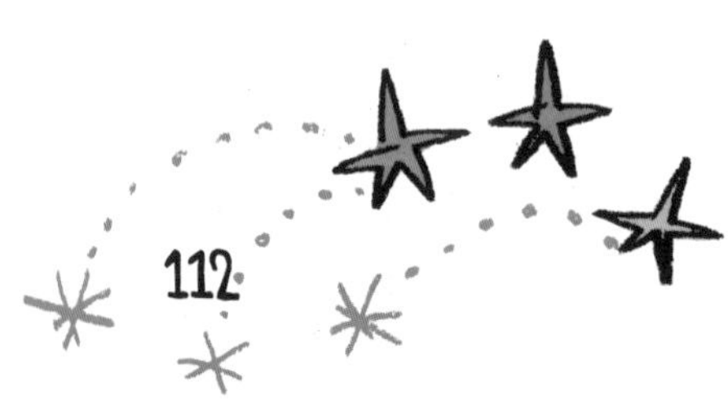

sauce, and a chocolate stick in each scoop was turned into three large sticky dollops of **mucky yucky, gloopy gritty mud!** Poor Adorabella had taken a huge slurp. And now she was **spluttering** and **spitting** out a mouthful of sludge!

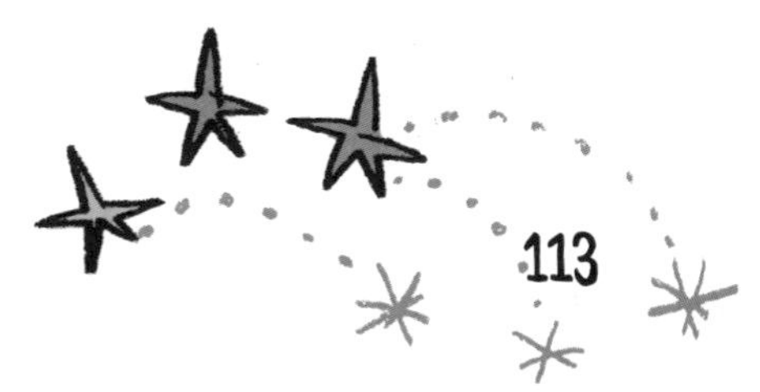

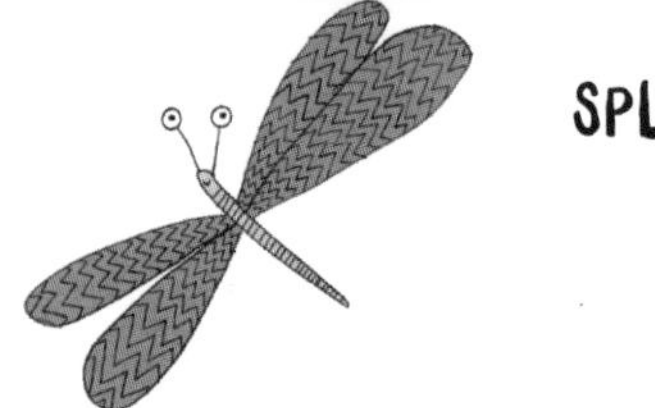

The Fairy Godmother rolled her eyes, sighed deeply, and reached for her wand. Nixie giggled wickedly, a look of pure mischief on her grubby little fairy face.

'I'm probably going to get into loads of trouble for doing that!' she whispered to Willow, sitting down next to him to finish her own ice cream, 'but it was worth it!'

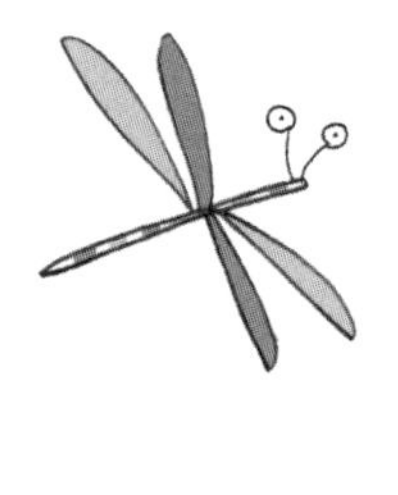

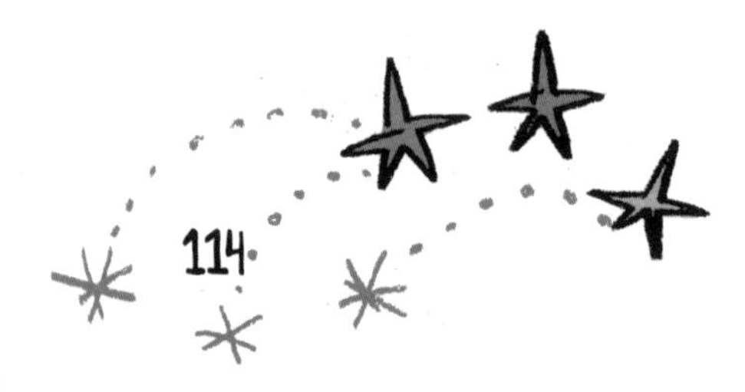

Acknowledgements

As ever – I owe a huge debt of heartfelt gratitude to:

Gaia Banks, my wonderful agent, because: 'A little magic can take you a long way.' *(Roald Dahl)*. Gaia – thanks for guiding me on such a magical journey.

Kathy Webb and Gill Sore, my fabulous editors at OUP because: 'One man's 'magic' is another man's engineering.' *(Robert A. Heinlein)*. Thank you both for your magical editing.

Ali Pye, the enormously talented illustrator, because: 'Using words to describe magic is like using a screwdriver to cut roast beef.' *(Tom Robbins)*. So it's just as well we've got your magical pictures!

And as always and forever:

Alfie, Bertie, Archie, and Annie (the original Bad, Bad Fairy) because: 'Love is the biggest magic of all.' Thanks for bringing the magic.

About the illustrator

I have wanted to illustrate books for almost as long as I can remember. When I was little I spent lots of time drawing and thinking up stories. I often got told off for 'having my nose in a book' or doodling when I was supposed to be helping my family—now I have to nag my own children for exactly the same reasons!

A Little Bit About Me . . .

I used to make children's television programmes for CBBC like Jackanory and The Story of Tracy Beaker. But now I'm writing books for children instead.

Which is great because it means I can spend much more time mucking about with my family and with Bramble, my daft dog. And I get to do lots of school visits, which I absolutely love. I'm also the author of the Harvey Drew books—comedy adventures set in outer space.

Ice cream sundae generator

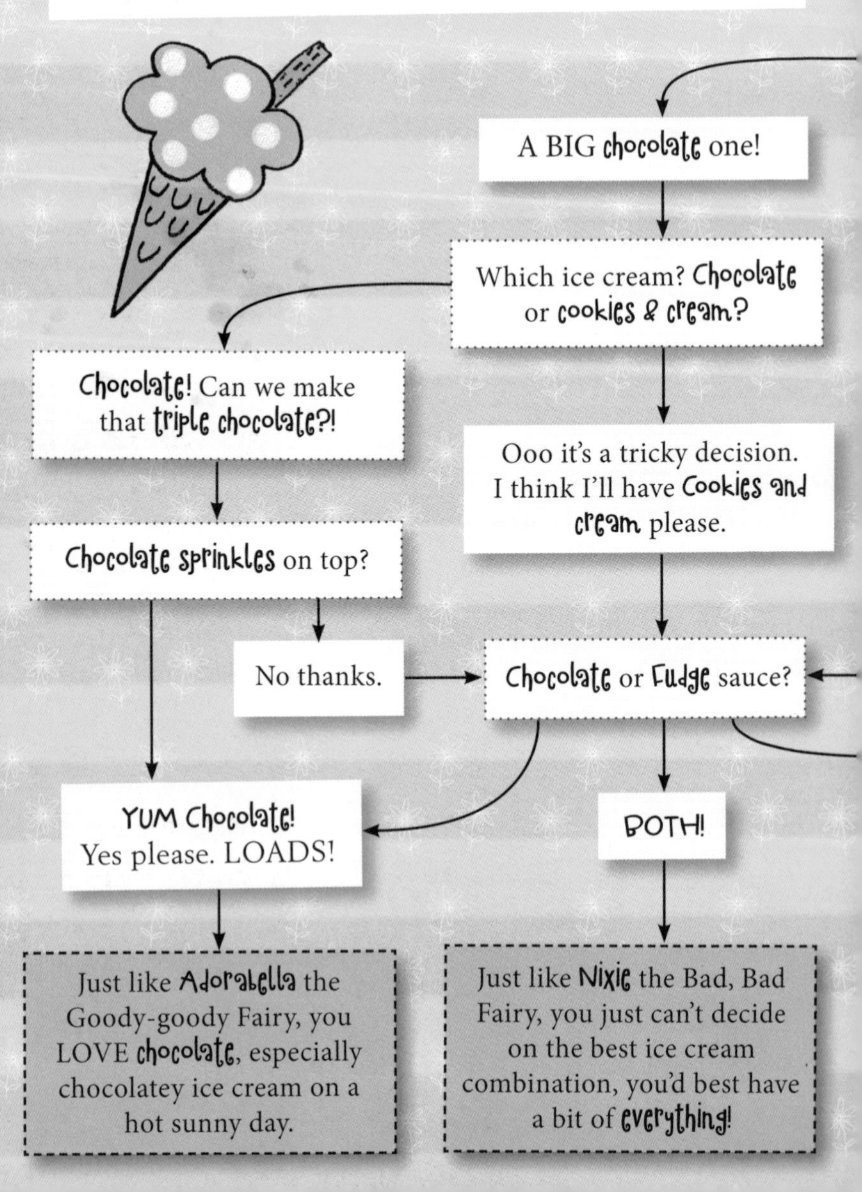

START
Which cone would you choose—a chocolate one or a plain one?
A DOUBLE plain one!
Which ice cream? Butterscotch or vanilla and strawberry?
Vanilla & Strawberry
Butterscotch
Raspberry sauce or Maple syrup?
Fudge
Maple Syrup
Raspberry sauce
Just like Willow the Tree Fairy, you have a sweet tooth, and love to build amazing dens.
Just like Briar the Flower Fairy you like fruity summery flavours, and love going strawberry picking.

YOU WILL NEED AN ASSISTANT, SO MAKE SURE THAT AN ADULT HELPS YOU.

Nixie's Fabulous Fizzy Fun

You don't need to have a wand to create uncontrollable fizzy foam, just follow Nixie's instructions to make your own bubbly volcanic eruption.

YOU WILL NEED:

- 1 CUP FLOUR
- ½ CUP SALT
- ½ CUP WATER
- A LARGE BAKING TRAY
- AN EMPTY BOTTLE
- WARM WATER
- WASHING-UP LIQUID
- FOOD COLOURING
- BAKING SODA
- VINEGAR

1 The first step is to create your volcano. To do this you'll need to make some salt dough. Add the flour and salt together in a bowl. Mix with a spoon, gradually adding the warm water.

2 When the mixture starts to come together, knead on a flat surface until the dough becomes springy.

3 Stand the empty bottle in the middle of the baking tray and mould your dough around it to create a volcano shape.

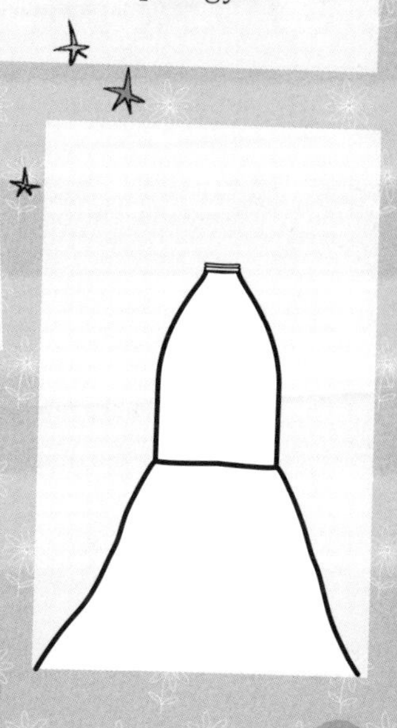

4 Your volcano is ready, now it's time to start the eruption. Fill the bottle halfway up with warm water and add several drops of food colouring.

5 Next, add a squirt of washing-up liquid, and a couple of spoonfuls of baking soda.

6 Are you ready for the fizzy foam? Then pour some vinegar into the bottle and watch the bubbles erupt!!

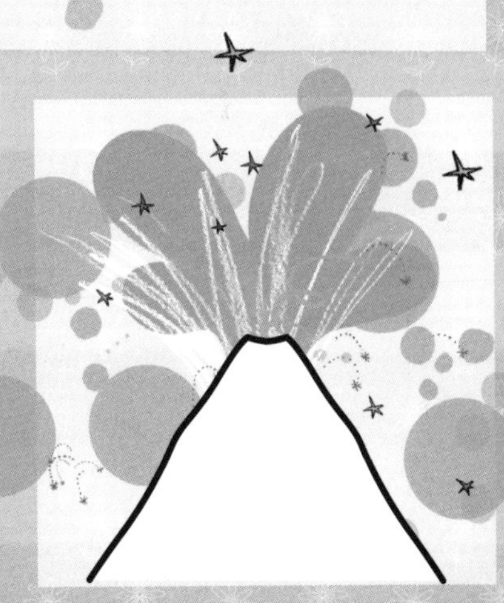

Get ready for more Nixie mischief in . . .

FIZZY FIREWORK FUN

THWACK!

A little wooden ball smacked into a hazelnut and knocked it onto the ground.

'Yahoo!' cried Nixie the Bad, Bad Fairy. She'd scored a hit with her very first throw! Her little black wings fluttered excitedly against her grubby red dress. She picked up a second ball, screwed one eye shut, took aim, and hurled the ball at another target on the hazelnut shy.

SMACK!

'Woohoo!' she cried, as another nut toppled to the ground!

'One more hit and you'll win a prize!' said the Palace Fairy who was running the stall.

Nixie's friends, Fizz the Wish Fairy, Fidget the Butterfly Fairy, and Twist the Cobweb Fairy, all

crossed their fingers for luck!

It was long after dark, and way after bedtime, but all the fairies were at the Fairyland Funfair and Fireworks display! The Fairy Queen held it every year at the Enchanted Palace. So tonight, Queen Celestine's enormous garden was jam-packed with dozens of hairy-scary rides, brightly lit fairground games with prizes, and colourful stalls of sweet smelling candyfloss and toffee apples. It was also full of flashing lights, blaring music . . . and noisy fairies! All laughing and screaming and yelling their heads off!

Nixie loved the fair—especially the dodgems, the spinning teacups, and the helter-skelter. But tonight the first thing she'd done was to rush over to the hazelnut shy to make sure she had the pick of the prizes! She couldn't decide between a giant blow-up hammer, a glow-in-the-dark water pistol, or an enormous bag of marshmallow twists . . .

But first, she had to knock one more hazelnut off its stand with her last ball. Squinting hard and

with her tongue poking out, Nixie took aim . . .

CRACK!

She hit the nut . . . but it didn't fall straight off! Nixie held her breath as it did a mighty wobble, and then . . . tremble, topple, teeter . . . PLONK!

'YES!' whooped Nixie as the nut finally fell off. She chose the marshmallows for her prize, ripped open the bag, shoved a couple into her mouth, and then offered some to her friends. Fizz and Twist helped themselves but Fidget had fluttered over to the hoopla stall to look at the prizes. One of them was a Glittery Butterfly Art Kit. Fidget loves anything arty and she really, really wanted it.

'Fidget!' called Nixie. But Fidget didn't answer. So Nixie called louder, 'FIDGET!' And then even louder 'FIDGET!'

But Fidget couldn't hear her—partly because the fair was so noisy, but mostly because Fidget was wearing a pair of huge fluffy earmuffs.

Nixie fluttered over and tapped her on the shoulder.

'Take them off!' she yelled. 'It isn't even that cold.'

'I'm not wearing them because I'm cold,' laughed Fidget, slipping the earmuffs off. 'It's because I don't like the noise of the fireworks.'

'But the fireworks won't be for ages yet,' pointed out Nixie and held out the sweet bag to her. So Fidget left her earmuffs round her neck and took a handful of marshmallows.

'Where shall we go next?' asked Nixie. There was so much to do!

Fizz wanted a go on the hazelnut shy, but Fidget said she'd rather go on the hoopla stall, and Twist wanted a toffee apple.

'I know! The dodgems!' cried Nixie, grabbing Twist and Fidget and hauling them after her.

'But what about my go on the hazelnut shy?' cried Fizz.

'You can do that later! Come on!' yelled Nixie over her shoulder.

So Fizz darted after her.

Love Nixie? Then we know you're going to enjoy reading about these fantastic characters too . . .